team picture

Dean Hughes

For the students of Metcalf Elementary, with best wishes,

Dean Hughes

ATHENEUM BOOKS FOR YOUNG READERS

Atheneum Books for Young Readers
An imprint of Simon & Schuster Children's Publishing Division
1230 Avenue of the Americas
New York, New York 10020

Book design by Angela Carlino
The text of this book is set in New Baskerville.

First Edition
Printed in the United States of America

10 9 8 7 6 5 4 3 2 1

Library of Congress Cataloging-in-Publication Data
Hughes, Dean.
Team Picture / by Dean Hughes.—1st ed.
p.   cm.
Sequel to: Family pose.
Summary: Trying to hold on to the newfound stability of his life in a foster
home, thirteen-year-old David worries about the growing moodiness of his
guardian Paul and the fluctuating fortunes of his Pony League baseball team.
ISBN 0-689-31924-X
[1. Foster home care—Fiction. 2. Baseball—Fiction.] I. Title.
PZ7.H87312Te   1996
[Fic]—dc20   95-52172

For Phil Sadler

chapter 1

David waited. All evening he watched old movies on cable, and the hours passed slowly, like the dripping of the rain onto the balcony outside. When midnight came, and then one o'clock, he told himself to expect the worst. And when the key finally sounded in the lock of the apartment door, David stood up, frightened and shaking. He told himself that he had always known this might happen sooner or later and that he couldn't let it get him down. But he didn't believe that. He believed that everything in his life was going to fall apart now.

Paul stepped inside the door, noticed that the TV was on, and then turned toward David. In the semidarkness, David couldn't see Paul's face, couldn't determine anything, but he saw something in the odd motion of Paul's hand, some loss of grace, as he slipped the keys into his pocket. "Why are you still up?" he asked, and David knew for sure. Paul had been drinking.

"I've been watching TV," David said.

"And waiting to check me out. Right?"

David shrugged.

"Well, sorry to disappoint you, David, but I'm not drunk. I had a couple of drinks and I'm fine. You—and everybody else—have it in your heads that all I have to do is take one drink and I'll be down in the gutter from then on, dead drunk. But I've got more control than that."

David couldn't believe this—not after all the promises. "Yeah, sure," he said. "And who cares what happens to me?"

"What's that supposed to mean?"

"Arnie is going to pull me out of here the minute he hears about this. You promised him that you would *never* have another drink."

"Ah, get off my back." Paul took a couple of steps away, as though he were heading down the hall to his bedroom, but then he turned back and walked toward David. He didn't stagger, but he moved slower than usual, as though walking in water. "I'll tell you what, David. I'll bet old Arnie takes a drink once in a while. Who doesn't? What did you think I was going to do tonight—sit there and drink soda pop?" Paul's voice was louder now, on the edge.

He pointed his finger at David's face. "You're always waiting for me to mess up. I think you *hope* for it."

"No, I don't."

"Why don't you give me a little credit, then? I could have let go, but I didn't. I had some drinks and then I stopped. What does that tell you?"

"It tells me I better pack my clothes. I'm going to be out of here."

Paul took a step forward, and now he was in David's face, his breath full of the alcohol. "You're going to call Arnie and tell him, aren't you?"

David wasn't going to do that. Arnie was his social worker, and David was actually terrified that the man would find out. "Don't talk so loud," David said. "You're going to wake up everybody in the building."

David wanted to leave now. He tried to step past Paul, but Paul grabbed him by the arm and held him.

"Don't run away. That's what you do every time I try to talk to you."

"I do not."

Paul jerked David's arm, pulling him square, so the two were face-to-face. "I know I'm not your father. I'm not trying to be. But you could learn a few things from me if you would listen."

"I do listen."

"No, you don't."

David let his breath blow out, loudly.

"Don't give me that disgusted look, David. Maybe I'm no college grad, but I've been around the block a few times and I've picked up some things. I could teach them to you."

David didn't know where this was coming from. Paul had never talked about any of this before. Maybe it was the alcohol.

"I'll tell you what you don't know. You don't know how to treat people. You don't have a friend in this world."

"I do too."

"No, David. You know you don't. Some of the guys on your team want to be friends with you, and you just turn and walk away from them. How many times have I talked to you about that?"

"That's my own business."

"Okay, fine. So what am I for? Just to feed you and buy your clothes?"

"That's not what I mean. I'm just saying I have all the friends I want. You don't need to worry about it." Suddenly David pulled forward, trying to get away.

Paul grasped his arm all the harder. "David, you've lived with me for a year and a half, and you're still a stranger. I don't know the first thing about you. You tell me nothing, and you listen to nothing I try to say to you. How are we supposed to get by together that way?"

"Don't worry about it. It's all over now anyway. And you're the one who messed it up."

"Hey, who do you think you're talking to?" Paul shouted into David's face. "I don't have to answer to you. I don't have to tell you where I've been or what I've been doing. That's none of your business." And then he shook his fist in David's face. "Right now, I feel like knocking you across this room."

David expected that fist to strike, but he didn't care. He could handle that.

"Get in bed right now. I told you when I left here tonight not to wait up, didn't I? I may not be your father, but I'm supposed to be in charge—whether you think so or not."

And so David went to bed. What he didn't do for a long time was go to sleep. He spent most of the night trying to think what he could do. What would happen to him if Arnie took him away from Paul? Would he end up with some foster family? Or maybe

4

get kicked around from one house to another for a while? Would he have to go through all that again? Paul's accusations kept slipping into his head, ringing so familiar, but he wasn't going to deal with any of that. Paul had no right to blame him for anything. Paul was the guy who had promised never to drink again. David clung to the hope that Paul would sober up and quiet down, and somehow this whole thing would blow over. But he knew better. Now that Paul had taken that first drink, this would be only the beginning.

When the jumble of thoughts finally cleared a little, and David was calming down enough to fall asleep, an image came into his mind. He remembered the day when he was lying in the hospital bed after the wreck, and his aunt told him that his parents and his brother had been killed. That was before the anger and the fear. It was a single moment when, like a magician's trick, the entire world was suddenly gone. He had turned, as much as he could with the tubes running into him, and he had looked at the beige-colored hospital wall, and it seemed that he saw in that blankness everything there was to see. He couldn't feel, couldn't think. All he knew was that there was nothing there, not one thing to hope for or even to care about. He was simply and absolutely alone.

Now David seemed to be looking at that wall again, and for an instant, he thought he was back in that hospital bed. He told himself that it wasn't like that this time, that he was older, that things were different. He opened his eyes and tried to see something in the darkness, just to reassure himself that he was in a new place and time. But in his mind was the same numbness, the same absence of emotion, and he remembered what would come next: all the grief and confusion and hatred. He just couldn't pass through that again. He had to be more in charge this time, and not let everyone else take over.

David did finally go to sleep, and then he slept well into the day. When he awoke and got up, Paul had long since gone to work. David took that as a good sign. But all day he waited and worried. And when Paul came home that afternoon, David watched for signs of what he could expect now.

Paul had stopped at a grocery store on the way home and had bought some frozen tortellini. He said very little, but he got to work, boiling the pasta and heating sauce in the microwave. He had also bought a loaf of garlic bread, which he stuck in the oven.

David liked Paul's meals all right, but he never understood why Paul didn't plan a few days ahead of time, and shop once a week or so. It was the same way he lived the rest of his life—a day at a time—and it kept David on edge.

David picked up his plate off the kitchen table and was about to leave. "Where are you going?" Paul asked.

"To watch TV."

"Just stay here a sec."

David put his plate down. He was actually relieved that Paul wanted to talk, but he was also a little frightened. He didn't want to start where they had left off the night before.

"David, a lot of what I said last night was stupid. I can't drink, and I'm not going to."

David nodded. He was not at all sure that Paul could keep his resolve, but at least he was no longer justifying himself.

"But some of those things I said last night needed to be said. You and I don't talk, David."

David didn't know what to say. Maybe that was true, but it wasn't something he had really thought about.

"I want you to have a good life, and I'm worried about the way you hide out from people. I've tried to talk to you about it once in a while, but I don't see any sign that you listen to me."

"You don't need to worry about it, Paul. I'm okay."

"David, you're not okay. Stuff is going on inside you . . ."

"I'm fine, Paul. You're the one who's upset all the time."

Paul toyed with his tortellini, flipping over the little doughnut shapes with his fork. He was a quiet man himself, and this sort of thing wasn't easy for him. "Okay. That's true, in a way," he finally said. "I'm having a hard time with a few things. And I have to deal with that myself. But you're a kid. It's my job to make sure you do okay with your life—and that worries me. I want to do this right."

"You're doing everything fine. Just don't drink and we'll be okay."

"It's not that simple, David." But Paul didn't seem to know what else to say. He began to eat again, slowly, and with little interest. David took a good look at him and noticed how much older he was getting to look. He was not much over forty, but his skin was taking on a drier, harder look, and his dark hair was laced with strands of gray.

David got up and walked to the sink. He dumped most of his food out and then washed everything down the garbage disposal.

"David, you need to eat more than that," Paul said. "You'll need your energy tonight. That's why I bought pasta. It's supposed to be the best thing to eat before a game."

"I'm not hungry." David opened the dishwasher and put his plate and utensils inside.

"Look, David, I know you're still upset with me about last night. And I know I messed up. But I had some things on my mind yesterday, and I was in a mood to let go. At least I didn't do that."

David knew it was better to keep talking right now even if he didn't want to. "What happened yesterday?" he asked.

"Well . . . you know how Ralph is. I know he put me on this morning shift just to see if I would quit. I don't like mornings and he knows it. But he figures he's the bell captain and he can do what he wants. I guess it's starting to get me down."

David had heard all this before, and he also understood the part that Paul wasn't saying. Paul knew it looked better if he didn't change jobs. He had taken David as his foster child, but only on a temporary basis. A guy who worked as a bellman at a hotel didn't have a very stable image, and so longevity in one job was one thing that could make him seem reliable.

"But then, something else happened yesterday," Paul said.

"What?"

"Melissa called."

David was leaning against the cabinet, looking down, but his head suddenly popped up. "Melissa? Where did she call from?" This was the best news David had heard in a long time.

"She's back in Seattle. In fact, she's been back for a while. She said she's been so busy she didn't get around to calling us for a while."

"Are we going to be able to see her?"

"Yeah. She said she'd get in touch soon."

David heard something in that, and for the first time he thought he understood what was going on with Paul. Melissa had once worked at the same hotel where Paul worked. She was only about half Paul's age, but Paul had been nuts over her.

"She . . . uh . . . seems to have her life together. She's going to college and everything. But I don't know, talking to her upset me a little, I guess."

"Why?"

"I don't know. I just . . . well, it's stupid. I guess I felt bad that she didn't contact us when she first got back—that she waited so long."

But David could read between all those lines, and he knew that Paul was hurting because he knew he would never have her. And David understood that better than Paul could ever imagine.

"So anyway, I messed up last night. But it could have been a lot worse. And it doesn't change anything. Okay?"

"Okay."

"And we need to talk things out more."

"All right."

But David didn't trust any of this. He would never really feel sure about things until he somehow had his life in his own hands and didn't have to depend on anyone else.

chapter 2

David had thrown two strikes, and now he wanted a strikeout, but he told himself not to get too eager. He accepted the catcher's signal and took a deep breath. Then he rocked, kicked, and threw a high and tight fastball. The batter jumped back.

David knew he had the guy set up. The catcher, Cory Stewart, signaled for a curve and David nodded. He gave the pitch his full motion, as though he were coming with his hard stuff again, but he snapped off a curveball. The batter leaned back as the pitch broke away from him and over the plate.

"Steee-rike three!" the ump barked.

David walked off the mound. One more inning to go, and his Pony League team—the Giants—had a 4 to 3 lead.

David could hear Paul shouting to him from the bleachers. "Way to fire, David! Keep it up." But David didn't want to think about Paul, or about last night, or about anything else. He just wanted to concentrate on his pitching.

James Gowans, the first baseman, ran past David and slapped him on the back. "Nice pitch!" he said.

David nodded. He wished that James and some of the other guys on his team could play consistent defense. They weren't that bad most of the time, but in the third inning they had fallen apart. They had given up three runs, all on errors.

David walked into the fenced-in area the players called the dugout. He walked to the end of the enclosure, dropped his glove in the corner, and stood by the fence. He reached up and took hold of the chain links, his hands on either side of his face, and he watched the Cardinals' pitcher warm up.

David had just turned thirteen and was actually the youngest boy on the team, but he was one of the tallest. He was wearing a purple shirt, which his shoulders filled very well. Still, something in his nicely trimmed hair, showing like a neat little border under his hat, and even the shyness in his brown eyes, made him seem younger than he was.

The Giants' second baseman, Jeff Wise, yelled, "Hey, Dave. Good job!" But David didn't look over at him. He wanted to stay focused. He still needed those three outs.

David had only started playing organized baseball the season before, but once he discovered what a strong arm he had, the game had become his passion. All through the wet Seattle winter he had gone out every day after school and thrown at a target. That target—in the shape of a strike zone painted on a retaining wall at the end of a little strip of lawn—had become the main focus of his life.

Control. That's what David had, and that's what pitching was all about. The Cardinals' pitcher didn't have it. David was sure that if his teammates had been more patient, worked for more walks, they could have had twice as many runs by now.

"Come on, Gabriel, take a couple of pitches," David whispered as the first of the Giants' batters stepped to the plate. But he didn't yell. The other guys on his team were doing enough of that.

Gabriel Sosa, the left fielder, went after the first pitch, reached for a ball outside, and bounced a slow grounder to the first baseman. He was an easy out.

Then Brent Schoenfeldt, the big kid who played in center, swung at a high fastball, and he popped the ball up. The catcher drifted a few steps to his right and made the catch in foul territory.

The last chance was Joey Curtis, who was a lousy hitter. He did let a few go by, but finally, with a two-and-two count, he struck out on a pitch that was nearly in the dirt. David couldn't believe how stupid it was to swing at a pitch like that. David was glad the bottom of the order was coming up for the Cardinals, but he told himself not to take any chances. He wanted strikeouts.

As he walked from the dugout, he heard all the chatter, his teammates yelling to him to blow the batters away. But David pitched best when he stayed away from a lot of emotion and thought of Cory's glove—like that target on the wall at home. And that's how he tried to think as he took his warm-up pitches.

The first batter was a small guy, a left-hander. He was a pinch hitter, but he didn't look like much of a threat. David decided to go after him. He started with a fastball, down in the strike zone. The batter swung late, but he got a piece of the ball. He bounced a slow grounder toward third base.

Dustin Ulrich, the Giants' third baseman, charged the ball and made a good pickup. David knelt to stay out of his way.

Dustin threw off balance—and hard. But he hurried more than he needed to, and the ball sailed high. James leaped, but he couldn't reach the ball. It rolled up the right-field line. The runner made the turn at first and raced over to second.

So already the tying run was in scoring position. David didn't look at Dustin, but he wondered why some players fell apart under pressure. If the guy had taken the time to set his feet, he could have had the out. Now the game could get away.

David went back inside himself. He had to get strikeouts. That was the only sure way.

The next batter was no one to worry about. David had struck him out twice already. David knew the guy would be hoping for a walk, so he fired a good fastball, down the middle. The second pitch was just as fat, and the batter took it all the way again—strike two.

Now the batter would be swinging. Cory signaled for the curve, but David shook off the sign. This guy couldn't hit his fastball, and David knew it. Why mess with anything else?

He didn't really blaze the ball, but he kept it low and maybe a little inside. The guy swung and missed by a good six inches. And now there was one out.

The Giants were all yelling—and so were the parents in the bleachers. David heard one of the Cardinals shout, "We can hit this guy. He's not that tough." But David didn't want to hear any of that. He liked the stillness that fell over the park just as he got ready to throw. He wished that the whole game could be played in silence.

The last batter in the lineup was coming up. David didn't worry about him. He threw three fastballs again. The kid swung late every time. He never touched the ball.

That took some pressure off. David only needed one more out.

But the situation was different now. This next batter was the lead-off hitter, a guy named Woodbury, and he already had two hits tonight. He had a nice, short swing, and he was smart enough to punch the ball out of the infield without going for the long ball. That's all it would take now. A single could score the runner from second and tie the game.

Everyone was yelling again—all the fans on both sides. David heard Paul above the others. "Come on, David. Just one more." But David told himself to think only of the catcher's mitt—the target.

He stepped away from the mound, tucked his glove under his arm, and he rubbed the baseball with both hands. The sun was setting, and the overhead lights had come on. David tried to breathe in some of the calm in the air. He told himself he could handle Woodbury this time. But the truth was, he was scared. He didn't want to come this far and then lose the game.

He went back to the fastball, down low. A little too low. The ump called it a ball.

Woodbury backed out of the box, swung his bat a couple of times, and then stepped to the plate and got set again. He was a fairly small kid, but quick. David could see the confidence in his face. The guy really thought he was going to get another hit.

David got the signal for a curveball, and this time he nodded. He took some speed off the pitch, and Woodbury swung early. But he nubbed the ball off the end of his bat. It trickled to the left side of the infield and died halfway between third base and the mound.

David charged the ball. He grabbed it, spun and set his feet. And then he threw a strike to first base.

Bam! It popped into James's glove and the game was over.

David had his win. He took a deep breath of relief. The Giants were now tied for first place in the league, with only one loss all year. And David had won every game he had pitched.

All the Giants' players charged toward David, surrounded him. "Good game!" they were shouting, and they were beating on his back. But David never knew how to handle that kind of stuff. It embarrassed him. "Thanks," he kept saying, but he didn't slap hands or yell. He just wanted to get to the bench so he could grab his duffel bag. He started in that direction.

Coach McCallister stepped in front of him, however. "Nice job," he said. The other players walked on by, and David waited. He could see that the coach had something else he wanted to say.

Coach McCallister was a quiet man, and David liked

him. He didn't do a lot of "motivating," but he knew the game, and he never stopped teaching.

"David, you pitched great," he said. He tucked his huge hands inside his belt, flat against his belly. He always wore a full uniform—the purple shirt and white pants—even though most of the coaches in the league didn't.

"Thanks," David said.

"How do you feel about that last play?"

David looked at the ground. "I don't know."

"Come on. Tell me what you should have done."

"I should have let Dustin take it, I guess. But I didn't want to take any chances."

"That's a tough throw for the pitcher. The third baseman is coming toward the ball, so that should always be his play."

"I know. But once Dustin makes a bad play, he gets nervous, and then he keeps messing up."

"Maybe. But it's still his play. When you take it away from him, you're telling him you *expect* him to mess up. In the long run, that hurts the team. Do you understand what I'm saying?"

"Yeah." And David knew the coach was right. But he couldn't really say he was sorry. He had gotten the out, and he wasn't at all sure that Dustin would have done that.

"Anyway, you pitched really well. Your control gets better every game. You've got a great future, David."

David liked hearing that, but he didn't say anything.

"Come on over. I've got a cooler full of sodas in my van."

"I have to go."

"Come on, David. Stick around a few minutes. You always take off as soon as the game is over."

"I know. But my dad has to get home."

"Can't you just stay five minutes?"

"Not really."

"Well, all right. Next week, we have games on Tuesday and Friday. And we'll practice on Thursday."

David nodded, and then he walked to the dugout. Most of the players were already heading toward Coach McCallister's van. Paul was waiting just behind the dugout. "The coach has some sodas for you," he said.

"Yeah, I know. But I don't want one. Let's go."

"No, David. You pitched a good game. Now enjoy the win with the guys."

"I don't want to. Okay?"

"Why?"

"What difference does it make?" David was already walking away. He walked to the end of the fence, which only extended a little past third base, and then he angled toward the parking lot, staying ahead of Paul.

By the time David reached Paul's old Buick, Paul had caught up. But he didn't say anything until he backed out of his parking spot and was driving down the street. "What's going on, David? Are you still upset about last night?"

"No."

Paul ran his hand over his hair, which he combed straight back, slick. He liked to wear turtleneck sweaters under his sports jackets, even on these summer nights. David had heard women say how handsome Paul was, and David supposed that he was, but he seemed to be clinging to an image he had taken on long ago—a look that was gone now. Paul always talked about the days when he had first become a bellman, when the hotels were classier, and the money was better. Maybe that's what he was feeling lately, that life had been better for him back then.

David looked out the window. The sun was almost gone now. It seemed to be sinking right into Elliott Bay. David got a glance, between buildings, at the orange reflection on the water. He and Paul lived on Capitol Hill, above the big buildings in downtown Seattle.

"You were great tonight," Paul said. "You should have had a shutout. Not one of those runs was earned."

And that's what David was thinking, too. He should have had a shutout, and yet, there at the end, his teammates almost blew the whole game for him. He wished he could strike out everybody. That would be the only sure way.

chapter 3

When Paul left each morning, David was usually still asleep. He could stay in bed as long as he wanted, but most mornings he got up by eight, poured himself a bowl of cereal, and then ate on the little balcony outside the apartment. This particular day, Monday, was one of those great Seattle summer mornings. It was cool but warming fast, with the haze burning off earlier than usual. The sky was going to be clear, and the water in Puget Sound would be as deep blue as the sky. David, however, was still not feeling great. After Paul had made such a point about the two of them talking more, he had had little to say all weekend, and David could sense how unhappy he was.

After breakfast, David got on his shorts and an old gray sweatshirt. He walked outside in his stockings and then put on his baseball cleats. He stood at the board he had imbedded in the grass—his own version of a pitching rubber—and he threw easily at first. He had read every book he could find on pitching theory, and he knew that he had to be careful with his arm while he was growing up.

He increased his speed gradually, and he worked on hitting certain spots. After he threw fastballs for a while, he tried to break his curve into the target. He knew better than to throw a lot of curveballs, since they were hard on his elbow, but he threw ten or so and then went back to the fastball.

He was pumping the ball pretty hard when he heard someone say, "You sure make a lot of racket out here every morning. How am I supposed to sleep?"

David knew the voice. It was the red-haired girl from upstairs. He didn't turn around. He wound up, kicked, and let go with a real heater. The ball cracked against the wall, above the target, and to the right. As it bounced back toward him, he had to take a couple of steps to his right to field it. He was embarrassed that he had thrown so wildly.

"Maybe you shouldn't sleep all day," he said.

"Why? I watch TV all night, so I *have* to sleep in the day."

David still hadn't looked at her. But she wasn't much to look at. She wore shorts most of the time, and she had long freckled legs, skinny as the neck of a baseball bat. She had moved into the apartment complex a couple of weeks ago. David had noticed that she had an older, prettier sister, and a mom, but apparently no dad who lived with them.

David fired another pitch, this time with a little less power on it, but he hit his target, very near the center.

"You actually hit that thing most of the time, don't you?"

"Yup."

"Wait—I think I know this story."

"What story?"

"You have a dream. You're going to make it to the *big show*, and you're willing to pay any price to get there. You work every day, rain or shine, and finally, you make it to the *bigs*." She said all this with fake passion, in a voice that was rather husky even when she wasn't forcing it.

David was still looking at his target, holding the ball, and he was trying not to smile.

"You become rich and famous, and hot women are after you, but deep down, you're not really happy. You get hooked on cocaine, and your life goes down the toilet."

David finally turned and looked at her. He tried to stop smiling. "What are you talking about?"

"I saw the whole thing in a movie. But don't worry. You finally discover what's most important in life. You buy a ranch in Montana and escape all the mess."

"Do I take one of those hot women with me?"

"Naw. They're too superficial for you. You go back to your high school sweetheart, to fresh air and wheat bread, and the two of you have lots of dogs and chickens and children."

David rolled his eyes, and then he turned back to his target. He wasn't interested in getting friendly with this girl. She was too weird. And she did look as though she had just gotten out of bed. She was wearing a faded green T-shirt, baggy shorts, and no shoes. Her hair was tied in a ponytail.

"So is that your story?"

"No. I'm going to leave the cocaine part out."

"Oh, I get it. You're really clean-cut and honest. I saw that movie too. You won't give in to the gamblers, and you end up losing your chance to play in the majors. That's a sad one. You better stick with the cocaine."

David couldn't pitch while she was talking. So he looked at her again, over his shoulder. She was smiling, showing pink braces. "I'll catch for you," she said, "if you don't want to throw at the wall all the time."

"No, thanks."

"Hey, I can catch. And I have a glove. I'll go get it."

"That's okay. I like to use the target."

"You really want to be a major leaguer, don't you?" She sounded serious.

"Sure. Who doesn't?"

"Me. I want to be nothing at all. I want to watch movies all night and sleep all day."

"That's a great goal."

"I know," she said, sort of wistfully. "So what's your name?"

"David Lambert."

"Actually, I knew that. But I figured if I started calling you by your name, you'd know I'd tried to find it out, and then you'd think I had this big crush on you. I also know you were in seventh grade last year, the same as me, and we'll be going to the same middle school. So now you're *sure* I have a crush on you, since I've been asking around about you. Right?"

David decided to throw a pitch.

As soon as he fielded the ball, however, she said,

"Don't you at least want to know what my name is?"

"Yeah. I've been dying to find out."

"Never mind," she said. And she was gone. David looked around to see her striding away, taking huge steps, with those baggy shorts flopping around her skinny legs.

David hadn't meant to hurt her feelings—but he didn't worry too much about it. He kept pitching. And he was just getting his concentration back when he heard the voice again.

"I decided to give you a second chance," she said. "I'm going to let you pitch to me, so I can show you how good I am, and then I'll tell you my name, if you ask nice."

David couldn't believe this. The strip of lawn was barely a full legal pitching distance. She was going to shorten that. But he didn't want to insult her again, and so he decided to throw a couple of pitches to her.

The girl crouched, with her knees spread wide and sticking way up—higher than her chin. She looked awkward, so David threw a sort of batting-practice pitch, about three-quarter speed. She caught the ball, and she threw it back with some pretty good zip on it. "Is that all the heat you've got?" she asked.

So David fired a good fastball at her.

It made a solid pop in her glove, and she didn't flinch. She came up throwing. David was impressed.

"I hate to say it, David, but you gotta throw harder than that or you'll never make it to the big leagues."

"Oh, is that right?" He reared back and steamed one. But the ball got away. The girl had to come out of her crouch and reach high. But she snagged the ball, stepped forward and tossed it back. "That wasn't bad, but you gotta throw your hard stuff with control. Let's see if you can hit my target this time."

"Do you play on a team or something?"

"I used to. But I quit."

"Why?"

"It was interfering with my busy schedule."

David laughed. He had to admit, this girl was all right in her own strange way. He kept throwing and she caught everything. But just when he was deciding this was a good thing he had going, she stood up and said, "Okay, that's all I can take."

"What?"

She pulled off her glove and raised her hand. Even from that distance, he could see that her palm was red. "Those babies really sting," she said. "You can *throw*." She walked toward him. "So do you want to know my name now?"

"Sure. Why not?"

"Well, don't act like it's a big thrill."

"Okay. I won't."

"Maybe I shouldn't tell you. If I had any cool at all, I wouldn't." Her face was flushed now, the color blending in with her freckles. She actually didn't look too bad that way.

David was smiling. "I *really* want to know," he said.

"Yeah, right. Well . . . call me Lynn. Lynn Mower."

"Isn't that your name?"

"Yeah. Sort of. But it's actually Patty Lynn, and my family calls me Patty. But I don't like that. I'll let you be the first person to call me Lynn. That's what I'm going to tell people to call me at school this year."

"What's wrong with Patty?"

"It sounds so . . . prissy. And my dad always called me Patty Pickle when I was growing up. That's when I got sick of it."

"I like that even better. 'Pickle' sort of fits you."

"I never should have told you that, huh?"

"Probably not." But then David asked, "Is your mom divorced? I never see your dad around."

"So do you watch me all the time or what?"

"No. I just—"

"I think *you* are the one with the crush. This is like that movie where the guy is in love, but he doesn't know how to say it. I can't think how it turns out, though. I think they get married. It's a dumb old movie—not very believable."

"I like old movies."

"You do? Or are you just trying to impress me because you have such a big crush on me?"

"I like old movies."

"Well, well. I have a TV, you know," she said, in a sexy voice. "You could come on up and watch with me some time."

David was suddenly flustered. He was afraid he had given this girl the wrong impression.

She seemed to see the confusion in his eyes. "Never mind," she said. "I'm doing what I always do. I talk too much. Don't worry. I won't bother you." Suddenly she was striding away again, taking those long steps. David was left wondering what had happened. And yet, the next morning, he found himself watching for her, hoping she would show up with her glove again.

She didn't appear, but just as David was about to quit pitching that morning, he saw Arnie drive into the parking lot. David really didn't want to see him right now, but he did seem pleasant as he waved and then walked over. He chatted with David for a minute or two before he said, "How is Paul doing?"

"Fine." David tucked his baseball glove under one arm, and he tried to act relaxed.

Arnie was a balding young man who wore little round wire-rim glasses. "You have no problems with the way he's treating you?" he asked.

"Nope. Not at all."

"I hope you're not covering for him."

"What do mean?"

"My office got a call on Friday. One of your neighbors heard him screaming at you the night before. Late at night. She didn't know whether he hit you or not, but she heard him threaten to knock you around."

"No way, Arnie. That's probably old Mrs. Pearson, next door. She gets everything mixed up."

"Are you saying none of that happened?"

"Paul got upset with me, and he chewed me out. But it was no big deal."

"What was he upset about?"

"I don't remember. It wasn't anything important."

"In the middle of the night?"

David could feel his face getting hot. He tried to sound offhanded when he said, "'Middle of the night' could be ten o'clock to Mrs. Pearson. She goes to bed before dark."

"Did he hit you?"

"*No!* He's never done that. And he won't."

"Had he been drinking?"

"No," David said again, but with less force.

"David, tell me the truth. This is really important."

"Paul doesn't drink anymore."

"Not ever?"

"No."

"David, I have to file a report. I need to know the exact truth. Tell me why he was yelling at you."

"It was my fault. He told me I shouldn't stay up so late, and I started talking back to him and sassing him and stuff. We talked it all over the next day, and everything is okay now."

"David, this puts me in an awkward spot. You've been with Paul a year and a half now. But I set this up on a temporary basis. I have to keep justifying a placement like this."

"Why?"

"It's not our usual sort of arrangement. Paul's a divorced guy who works as a bellhop. That's not—"

"He's had the same job for a long time."

"I know. But if my boss had known that Paul has a history of drinking problems, you never would have been placed with him. And now I've got to file a report about this new situation."

"Why? Nothing happened."

"I still have to write it up. There was a complaint, and I have to check it out. I've got to interview the lady who called. And I need to talk to Paul. Is he home?"

"No. He's working day shifts now."

"What time does he get off?"

"Three."

"I'll have to stop back later, I guess."

"Arnie, I don't want to leave Paul. Don't turn in some stupid report that's only going to cause problems. Just throw the paperwork away."

"No. I can't do that." Arnie reached out and put his hand on David's shoulder. "Look, I don't want to pull you out of here. But if Paul is drinking, or if some kind of abuse is going on, I've got to protect you. That's my job."

"He *doesn't* abuse me. He goes to my baseball games and everything. He's just like a dad to me."

"Well, all right. That's good to hear. Are you getting good grades in school?"

"Yeah. Very good."

"Okay. Just keep it that way. As long as you're happy and doing well, I can probably keep you here. But it's always going to be temporary. Adoption isn't going to happen."

"That's okay."

"Do you ever hear from your relatives?"

"My one aunt sent me a Christmas card."

"Maybe she's ready to take you now."

"She didn't want me in the beginning. Why would she want me now?"

"Things change. When your case comes up for review, my boss will want me to check with all your relatives again."

"They don't care about me."

Arnie took his glasses off and rubbed the bridge of his nose. "Look. I'll make some calls. But I won't talk your relatives into anything. And I'll try to play down this incident the other night."

"Okay." David nodded.

Arnie patted him on the shoulder again. "You look good, David."

But then Arnie walked toward the building, and David knew he was going in to talk to Mrs. Pearson. He hoped she wouldn't be too convincing.

chapter 4

David worried all day. What if Arnie talked to Paul before David could tell him what to say? If Paul came up with a different story, Arnie would get suspicious. Or what if Paul told the truth?

By afternoon, David had built the concerns up in his mind enough that he decided he would walk downtown to the Jefferson Hotel, catch Paul at quitting time, and then tell him the situation as they drove home together. He didn't want Arnie to show up just as Paul got home, and catch him off guard.

The walk was fairly long, but David was glad to have something to do, and in his anxiousness, he left too soon. When he reached the hotel, Paul still had twenty minutes until quitting time. David decided to wait outside. He didn't know whether the manager would want him hanging around in the lobby.

At about a quarter to three, David's friend Betty, the

evening desk clerk, showed up for work and spotted David. She grabbed him and pressed him against all her softness. And then she took him inside with her.

David couldn't walk into the lobby of the Jefferson without remembering the desperate days when he had run away. After his family had been killed, David had eventually ended up with a stiff, reserved couple named Poulter. They had done their best, but they had come to dislike David, and Mr. Poulter had accused David of being cold and distant. David had known he was heading back into the system, to be shuffled around from one family to another again, and so he had taken off. He had planned to get to California, to survive on his own and not to let anyone control his life again, but he had needed a warm place to sleep, and he had sneaked into the hotel. That's when Paul had found him.

Paul had let David stay in the hotel for a while, but he had needed help to pull that off. And so Elaine and Rob, the night workers on the front desk, had gotten involved, and then Betty. And Melissa, who was a cocktail waitress, had let him stay at her apartment for a time. But it was Paul who had stuck with David.

"David, you grow another half a foot every time I see you," Betty was saying. "And you're such a beautiful kid." She grabbed him and hugged him again.

David pulled away as quickly as he could, but Betty only laughed about that. She stepped behind the counter and said hello to an older man who was finishing the morning shift on the front desk. David knew that the man's name was Harold, but he didn't really know him.

About then, Ralph, the bell captain, came around the corner. He had obviously just arrived for work; he didn't have his uniform on. "Hey, kid, how ya doing?" he said. "Are you still with Paul?"

"Yes." Ralph could never remember David's name, but he also seemed surprised every time he saw David—as though he never expected Paul and David to stick it out.

"You're almost as tall as I am. What's Paul been feeding you?" Ralph held his upper lip stiff as he laughed. David had seen his teeth, how decayed they were, but Ralph always tried to hide that. David couldn't believe that after all this time he still hadn't been to a dentist.

"Paul's done a wonderful job," Betty said. "I always told you he would."

Ralph shrugged. "Maybe Paul can teach him to think he's better than everybody else," he said. "That's one thing he knows all about." Then he walked away, chuckling to himself.

"What's that all about?" David asked Betty.

"Oh, Ralph is just being Ralph. The guy is jealous because Paul has class, and people like him. They tip him *twice* as much as they do Ralph, and it drives Ralph crazy."

Betty opened the little door and walked behind the desk, and she continued to talk to David until Paul got off an elevator and spotted David. He looked surprised. "What's up?" he asked as he walked over.

"I walked down. I thought I'd get a ride home with you."

Paul seemed to know that something was going on.

But he didn't ask. As soon as Ralph came out to the lobby with his uniform on, Paul went to the bellman's room and changed. Then he waited until he and David were in the car before he finally asked why David had walked downtown.

"Arnie came by this morning," David said. "Somebody called his office—Mrs. Pearson, I think—and said you were yelling at me the other night."

"Oh, brother. Did you tell him I'd been drinking?"

"No." David had been looking at Paul, but now he turned forward and looked out the front window. "I told him you *never* drink. I lied."

"You didn't have to do that."

"I made up a story, but it's sort of true. You better say the same thing. I told him that you were trying to get me to go to bed and I got sassy with you. That's why you were mad."

"You don't have to cover for me, David," Paul said. "I don't want you doing that."

"He's going to talk to you, Paul. If you tell him you were drinking and yelling, he'll put it in a report. Mrs. Pearson heard you say you were going to knock me across the room."

"I'm going over to Arnie's office right now," Paul said. "I'll see if I can straighten this out."

"Okay, but don't—"

"David, I'll handle it. All right?"

At Arnie's office, however, Paul did the worst thing David could think of. "You might as well know," he said. "I slipped up that night. I had a few drinks. But that's the first time since I've had David. And I didn't go off on a binge. I had three drinks, and then I quit."

David felt sick. He had no idea why Paul was doing this.

"Paul, I can't believe you did that," Arnie said. "You can't drink socially. You're an alcoholic."

"I know that. I've let some things get to me lately. But I've got my head back on straight. It won't happen again."

"The person who reported you said you threatened to hit David."

Paul paused and thought. "I yelled at him. But I didn't touch him. I never have. You don't have to worry about that."

"Well," Arnie said, "I'll put all this in the report. I can live with it myself for right now—considering how well David seems to be doing—but I don't know what my boss will say."

Arnie sat and wrote on the report for a minute or so. David kept watching Paul, who seemed nervous. "I don't want something like this to mess us up," he told Arnie. "I've really done my best. I want to keep David."

"I know, Paul. But this placement was based on your promise that you wouldn't drink at all. I think you've been good for David, but it just *can't* happen again. And David, you've got to be honest with me from now on."

"He will," Paul said. But David looked away.

"Listen, Paul," Arnie said, "why don't you walk down the hall with me for a moment? I'll introduce you to my boss. It might be good for him to get to know you."

"Are you going to bring this new thing up?"

"No. He doesn't know anything about it at this point. I'm just thinking it might be good for him to know what you're like. It's always better than just reading something on paper."

"Well, sure. That's fine with me. Do you want David to come along?"

"Uh . . . maybe not. Let's talk to him alone. He'll probably want to ask you how David's doing." Arnie got up and stepped to a large filing cabinet. He looked for a time, and then slipped the report into a file. "We'll be back in a few minutes, David. You can just sit here, if you want."

"Okay," David said, but he wondered what Paul might say now. Why hadn't he just kept his mouth shut?

As soon as Arnie shut the door, David thought of the report. He didn't want anyone, ever, to see it. And this was his chance. Reports got lost all the time. Why couldn't this one get misplaced?

It took David a couple of minutes to get up the nerve, but he stepped to the file cabinet. He opened the drawer and fingered through the files until he found his folder. He pulled out the report and then he walked quickly to the door. He peeked out, saw that Arnie and Paul were not in view, and then he hurried down the hall to the lobby. He wadded up the report as he walked, and he tossed it in a trash can.

He hurried back, shut the door to the office, and sat where he had been before. He was breathing hard, and already he wondered whether he had done the right thing. But he felt better to have done something. He couldn't stand to think of some stupid report lurking in a file, waiting to mess up his life.

When Arnie and Paul got back, Paul seemed in a good mood, more relaxed. Arnie was acting more comfortable too. David figured the chat with the boss had gone well.

Once they had walked outside, however, David said, "Why did you do that, Paul? You didn't have to admit to all that stuff."

"David, I've lied enough in my life. I'm playing this straight. I wouldn't have called and reported myself, but since he knew about it, I wasn't going to lie to the man."

"I wish you had."

Paul came to a sudden stop. David took another step or two, and then he turned and looked back. "David, I'm not a con man. I'm not *Ralph*. And you're not going to be either. Don't ever lie for me again."

"Then don't drink again."

Paul didn't say anything. But David saw the hurt in his eyes. He walked on to the car and got in. David got in the other side. Paul started the car and backed out. He was going back into that silent state he had been in so much lately. David didn't want that. "Paul, I'm scared," he said. "I worry about what's going to happen."

"I know. I'm sorry I put you in a situation where you felt you *had* to lie for me."

That sounded better. But David thought about the report. Paul would be mad if he ever found out about that, but David didn't care. He wasn't sorry he had gotten rid of it.

chapter 5

David's team had a game on Tuesday night. David wasn't pitching, but he played most of the game at third base. The Giants got six runs in the first inning and then coasted. David was glad for the win, but he had a hard time getting involved when he wasn't pitching. Paul did talk David into staying around after, long enough to drink a soda with the guys. He actually did like some of the players, but he never knew what to say to them. It was easier just to go home when the game was over.

The next morning David went outside to pitch at his target, as usual. But once he was finished he didn't have anything to do. He surfed through the cable channels with the TV remote until he decided there was nothing he wanted to watch. And then he took a book out onto the balcony, but he soon found that he was staring off at the city and the bay beyond.

He couldn't stop thinking about the report he had thrown away. He wondered when Arnie would look into that file the next time, and it worried him. He was also worried about Ralph trying to push Paul into quitting. He hated the idea that things were happening that he couldn't do anything about.

David had no idea what to expect from Paul now. Until lately, Paul had been gone most evenings, and that had been all right with David. Now, with Paul's new schedule at work, and with him coming to all David's games, Paul was pushing again, finding things wrong with David, trying to change him. And even though he said he wanted to talk more, when Paul talked about himself, he talked about his past. David knew that Paul had been married three times, that he had had two daughters with his first wife and another one with his second. His former wives and his daughters all lived in California. But Paul hadn't seen any of them for years.

All that didn't really affect David—except that Paul had so many regrets. When he talked, he sounded unhappy, and when he stopped talking, he looked depressed. And that was another worry.

So David stared out at the bay, but he seemed to be looking at that beige wall he knew so well, and he felt some of that old numbness begin to buzz in his head. It was so hard to see any kind of future he could count on. And then, as he did so often, he let himself drift into his favorite fantasy. He saw himself in a big baseball stadium, and he was standing on the mound, ready to pitch his first game in the majors. He had placed his foot on the pitching rubber, and now the crowd hushed, and only he, the catcher, and some nebulous batter existed. And then he began to throw, and each pitch was perfect. It glided from David's hand to the catcher's mitt as though guided by his will. The batter would swing and miss, or he would stand at the plate, baffled, and take called strikes. From time to time a batter might foul one off, but none of them ever put the ball in play.

One after another, every batter struck out. *Every* batter. "He did it! He did it!" the radio announcer would shout. *"He struck out every batter!* This is the greatest moment in baseball history!"

A perfect game was twenty-seven outs in a row. But David wanted the *perfect* perfect game. Nothing but strikeouts. And he did more than imagine it. He believed it. If he practiced every day, did everything right, he could find that perfect control he needed.

He never really thought about the media attention. He didn't even imagine his teammates hoisting him onto their shoulders. He just pictured himself overpowering batter after batter, and finally getting that last strikeout. And then, after the game, he pictured himself going home to *his* house, *his* family, where nothing was temporary, where no one was "foster" anything.

Most of this was sort of abstract. He never saw the children, never knew how many there were or what they looked like. He just felt the mood of this house, where everyone was happy—and nice to each other. Sometimes, however, he did see his wife, and he knew her face. He told himself, over and over, not to think about that. He didn't want to include anything in his little daydream that was impossible. But today, he allowed himself the luxury of picturing her. She didn't seem as remote as she had been for a long time.

David wasted his day, doing little, slipping into his daydream time and again, until finally he couldn't resist going back outside to practice some more. He concentrated hard, pushed other thoughts from his mind. He was still throwing when he saw Paul drive into the parking lot in his old blue Buick. Another car, a little white Toyota, drove in at the same time and pulled into the parking spot next to Paul's. David knew Paul would come over and chat with him, and so he tossed the ball again, hit the target just a few inches to the right of where he was aiming, and then fielded the ball as it bounced back across the grass.

David glanced over at Paul, but then he saw someone getting out of the other car: a woman in white shorts and a red shirt. For a moment, he didn't dare think it, but he saw her flip her hair back, with one hand, and he knew that motion, even knew the hair. It was Melissa.

David started walking, slowly, unsure what he would do when he got to her. But she was walking toward him, fast, and her beautiful hair—lighter now, it seemed, almost blond—was blowing back. David stopped in front of her, and she grabbed him and hugged him, her arms wrapped all the way around him. David kept his own arms to his sides. He was too embarrassed to take hold of her.

"David, you're so tall. I can't believe it. It's like you jumped from being a little boy to a young man, all at once." It was the best thing she could have said. But David couldn't think of one thing to say to her. She took hold of his shoulders and held him back a little.

"And you are *so* handsome. You have such *dreamy* brown eyes. My gosh, the girls must go nuts over you."

"How do you like being back in Seattle?" he asked, partly to change the subject.

"I love it. Did Paul tell you? I'm going to college?"

"Yeah. That's what he said."

David knew all about Melissa's past. She had grown up in Minnesota, and she had run off with an older guy when she was only about seventeen. The man had married her, but then he had walked out, and she had survived on her own in Seattle for a few years. She had decided to go back to Minnesota not long after David had moved in with Paul, and David had expected never to see her again.

David took a long look at her, and then he looked away. There was something about the softness of her skin, the dark blue of her eyes, the arch of her top lip—it was all so perfect. It always embarrassed him to look her straight in the eyes. He was sure she could tell what he was thinking.

"Oh, you sweetheart," she said. "It's so good to see you." And she pulled him to her again. He was as tall as she was now, and he could feel her breasts against his chest. He pulled back rather quickly, embarrassed.

"Throw a couple of pitches," Paul said. "Show her what an arm you have."

David shook his head. "Not now," he said. And what he knew was that he would probably miss the whole wall. And so they walked inside, and Paul got some Cokes out of the refrigerator. Then they all went out to the balcony, where the sky was beautiful, and David sat there, dazzled, hardly speaking at all.

Paul told David that Melissa had shown up at the hotel that afternoon, at quitting time. "I meant to come and see you guys as soon as I got back in town. But I've been *so* busy. I'm having to work my little buns off, just to pass my classes."

David looked away, embarrassed again. He was trying to think how old she must be now. Probably twenty-five or twenty-six.

"So tell me what you've been doing since I saw you, David," she said.

"I don't know. Going to school. Playing baseball."

"Are you getting good grades?"

"Yeah. Pretty good."

"Hey," Paul said, "tell her what happened last term."

"I made the honor roll."

"All right," Melissa said, and she reached across the little glass table and patted him on the arm. "I thought you used to have trouble with your reading."

"Yeah, I used to. But not anymore."

"What happened? Did Paul help you?"

Paul laughed. "That's a joke," he said.

"I just started trying harder, mostly."

"Oh, David, that's so wonderful. And you're this big baseball star. Paul was telling me all about it."

David shrugged.

"Paul's been good for you, hasn't he? And you've been good for Paul. You guys needed each other."

David nodded, barely, and looked back out at the city.

"I'm coming to see some of your games. In fact, I'm coming on Friday. I have the night off. Paul and I already talked about that."

David felt his breath catch. But he liked the idea. He was pitching that game. Maybe he could throw a shutout, or strike out a lot of batters.

"I can't believe you're the same person. When you stayed with me that time, you were this precious little boy. Now you're so *stunning*—like some teenaged movie star." She laughed. "But I won't say that anymore. I'm making your face red." She touched his arm again.

After that Melissa talked about her time in Minnesota. She said she had resolved things with her parents, who had been so disappointed when she had run off all those years ago. "But I love Seattle," she said. "I had a pretty good job at home, and I thought about going to college somewhere out there. But Seattle just seems more like home to me now. And I'm too independent. Mom wanted to make my decisions, and I got really tired of that."

Paul talked more than usual. He always seemed to be more alive, more open, when Melissa was around. He watched her constantly, the same as David did. He kept coming back to David, telling about his baseball, but he also told Melissa, "This whole thing hasn't been that easy."

"Every family has its problems," Melissa said. "But you guys have done great together."

"Well, David's not always so sure. I've been going through a hard time lately, and I've been kind of moody."

"But you aren't drinking, and that's a big accomplishment."

Paul glanced at David. "Don't worry," Paul said.

"David is the best thing about my life right now. I wouldn't have anything, if he weren't with me."

It was the gentlest thing Paul had said in a long time. David was warmed by the words, but he also saw the sadness come into Paul's eyes. After Melissa was gone, when her sweet smell was still lingering in the apartment, David watched Paul sink back into himself. He hardly said another word the rest of the night.

chapter 6

On Friday night David was pitching against a team called the Braves. It was a decent team, with a couple of pretty good hitters, but it wasn't a lineup he worried all that much about.

Melissa kept her promise. She arrived just as David was warming up before the first inning. David saw her find Paul and sit by him, and then he heard her shout, "All right, David. Go after 'em!"

David took a long breath and tried to calm down. But his final practice pitches sailed high as he tried to put something extra on them. All week he had been thinking about this moment, and he had let himself imagine that he could strike out every batter. He knew that was dumb, that he wasn't ready to do that, but the fantasy had come back to him, over and over.

When the first batter stepped into the box, David tried to calm down and find his focus. He had to concentrate on the tunnel of space between him and that catcher's mitt. He told himself to forget about strike-outs. If he could put his pitches where he wanted them, the batters wouldn't have a chance.

His first pitch was hard but up a little high. Still, the batter swung, and swung late, not ready for David's speed.

David came back with another fastball and tried to catch the inside corner. The batter backed away, and the umpire called the pitch a ball. David thought he should have had the strike, but he didn't worry about it. He threw a change-up, and the poor batter was so far out in front of the pitch he almost fell down.

And now David came with his heat. Again, the ball took off a little, but the batter was overpowered. He stuck his bat out, late, as the ball popped into Cory's mitt.

Strike three. One away.

And Melissa, her voice rising high with excitement, yelled, "Way to whiff him! Keep it up, David." David loved it.

He pumped a fastball, hard and away. The batter got a piece of the ball and lifted a pop-up to the first-base side, in foul territory. David almost wished the ball would drift out of play—so he could still go after the strikeout. But James got under the ball near the fence, and he reached up and made the catch.

That was all right—better, in a way, David told himself—but he was already thinking that he could still get a no-hitter. And when he bore down and struck out the last batter, for an easy one-two-three inning, he felt sure that he could do it.

When David walked into the dugout he heard about Melissa immediately. Brent grabbed David by the arm and said, "Hey, Lambert, who's the *babe?*"

"What are you talking about?" David said, but he knew exactly what Brent meant.

"Who's the girl up there yelling for you?" Brent was a big round-headed kid. He was looking up at the bleachers like someone leering at a dirty picture.

"She's just a friend of mine," David said.

"Is she your dad's girlfriend or something?"

"No. She's a . . . family friend."

Jeff Wise, the second baseman, was listening to all this. He was a short kid, and so he stepped up on the bench to get a look at Melissa. "Wow. I wish she was *my* friend," he said. "She could come over to my house and play any time she wanted."

"Lay off," David told him. "She's nice."

"Hey, I believe it. I'll bet she's *very* nice."

"Just shut up. Okay?"

David walked to the end of the dugout. He stood at the fence and gripped the wire. The guys were all laughing now, and some of them were standing on the bench, stretching their necks to get a look at her.

The Giants got their lead-off runner on base, but the team didn't score, and it wasn't long until David was walking back to the mound. He focused on Cory's mitt, and the rest of the scene, even the batter, faded into a hazy frame, just the clouded edges of a sharp picture.

He rocked forward, back, and then kicked his leg as his body turned. He felt in command. He kept the ball a little off the plate, outside, and the batter chased it, just as David had hoped he would. Then he came inside with a fastball, off the plate again. The batter backed away.

Now the curve, and it broke sharply over the plate and down. The batter swung hard, but he was bailing out. David saw a puff of dust as he heard Cory's mitt pop.

He loved that sound, that little image.

He went to his hard stuff again, this time on the inside edge. And the batter seemed locked in place. The pitch was there, but he never got the bat in motion.

The ump showed off a little, swung his right arm in the air, and bellowed, "Steeee-*rike* three."

David really had it going now. He struck out the next two batters just as easily. He had six straight outs, and he was in a zone, sure that no one could get to him tonight.

He was leading off the next inning, so he got a bat and he walked to the on-deck circle. He took some easy swings, timing the pitcher's warm-up throws. And then, when the ump waved him into the box, he stepped up to the plate and waited, calmly. The first pitch was high, and he let it go by. But he seemed to know where the next pitch would be: belt-high and over the plate. He took a smooth swing, timed it perfectly, and lashed the ball into center field. He rounded first, going hard, but he decided to hold up even though he might have had a chance to stretch the hit to a double.

Chase Wright, the shortstop, came up after that and hit a long shot in the gap between center and right field. David scored from first, and Chase made it all the way around to third. And then Cory knocked him in with a sacrifice fly.

The Giants got another hit after that, but they only got the two runs in the inning. David didn't care that much. He felt that he had all the runs he needed.

The first batter in the top of the third inning was the Braves' second baseman. He was an awkward-looking kid with a bent-over stance. He swung and missed on a fastball, but then Cory called for a change-up. David actually thought it was the wrong pitch, but the batter looked bad, and so he didn't worry.

But a slow pitch was just the thing for this guy. He got his bat around in time. He didn't connect all that well, but he hit a little looper that arched toward right field. Jeff chased it, hard, but the ball dropped just beyond his reach and the batter had himself a single.

Suddenly, the no-hitter was gone, and David was really mad at himself. If he had stayed with his fastball, the guy never would have had a chance.

He did throw fastballs to the next two batters, and he got his strikeouts. But then the lead-off batter came up for the second time. The guy was a pretty good hitter, and he was very fast.

David knew he had to be more careful than he had been with the last two batters. He stayed a little outside with the first pitch, trying to bait the batter. But the guy didn't swing. And then David got the ball inside on the second pitch. Ball two.

David really didn't want to walk anyone. He felt the tunnel disappearing, all the surrounding sounds and pictures coming back into his head. "Fire it in there, David!" Paul was yelling.

David came down the middle with the next pitch—but he had aimed, and he didn't get his usual speed on the ball. The batter spanked it hard to the left side.

Still, Chase should have handled the ball at short-stop. He broke to his right, and he stabbed at the ball, backhanded, but it hit his glove and glanced off. The ball rolled up the left-field line, and the runner from first rounded second and headed for third.

David ran to back up the play at third. Gabriel had chased down the ball by now, and he had plenty of time to throw out the runner. But he must have heard everyone yelling, and he spun quickly and hurried his throw. The ball came in off line and got past Dustin. David dove for it but couldn't reach it. The ball shot across the infield, and before anyone could get to it, the runner had headed home. He crossed the plate, standing up.

David was furious. He knew he had made a bad pitch, but the ball never should have gotten out of the infield—and certainly a run never should have scored.

The problem now was that the other runner had gone all the way to third on the error. David knew he had to get a strikeout or the score would be tied. He just couldn't take a chance on his teammates.

David was more aware of the Braves' bench now. All those guys had come alive and were really whooping it up. So David went inside himself. He shut everything out. He felt for that tunnel, that focus. His first pitch was out over the plate, popping with speed. The batter waved at it and missed. And David knew he had the guy.

He threw another fastball, kept it down at the knees. The batter let it go by, and the ump shouted,

"Strike two!" And then David pumped one hard and up. The guy took a wild swing, and that was it.

After that, David was confident again. He got out of the inning, and he walked back to the dugout, but he stayed away from everyone, trying not to listen to the things they were shouting. Each time he walked back to the mound, he found that place where only he and the catcher existed. Not every out was a strikeout, and he gave up one more hit, but David mowed the Braves down. And the Giants scored five more runs.

So he got his win, 7 to 1, and when he walked off the field, Melissa and Paul had already come down to the fence. "You were *fantastic!*" Melissa yelled to him.

David heard some of the boys laugh, and Jeff said, "Oh, Davey, you're my hero."

David left with Paul and Melissa, without staying around for any celebrating. Melissa took him and Paul in her car, and they drove to a fast-food place not far away. "My treat," she told them. "Get yourself the biggest hamburger they've got."

"I just want a milk shake or something like that," David said.

"Get one of those huge sundaes they sell here. With chocolate and nuts and everything."

"Okay," David said, and he laughed. He suddenly felt surprisingly happy—happier than he had been in a long time. The game had seemed messy to him—giving up those hits and even a run—but Melissa didn't seem to mind that. She kept telling him how great he was.

Paul picked a booth in the far corner of the place, and the three of them slipped into the red cushioned wraparound seat. Melissa was in the middle. "Oh, my gosh, everyone's looking over here," she said. "They're all saying, 'That woman is out with two handsome guys, and one of them is this studly baseball star.'"

"The *ace* of the team," Paul said, laughing more than he ever did, normally.

"Someday I'm going to strike out every single batter in a game," David said. But David was stunned that he had actually said the words. He had never admitted to his fantasy before.

"You'll do it, too," Melissa said. "You got most of them tonight."

"The coach told me that David can make it to the big leagues someday if he keeps working really hard," Paul told her.

"Wow! Really?"

David was embarrassed, but he liked the way Melissa was looking at him. She was smiling, the dimple by the side of her mouth showing, those beautiful blue eyes concentrating all their attention on him. David glanced over at Paul, but Paul was watching Melissa, and smiling, too.

chapter 7

The next morning David went out and threw a few pitches, just enough to loosen up. It was a Saturday morning, and Paul was sleeping in. David was about to go back to his apartment when he saw Cory Stewart ride into the parking lot on his bike. His catcher's mitt was hanging from the handle bars. Cory had come over a couple of times before, and the two of them had played a little catch. David liked Cory better than any of the other guys on the team.

"Hey, Cory," David said. "Over here."

Cory pumped his bike on over, and then he laid it down next to the curb. "Do you want to throw some pitches?" he asked.

"I've probably done all I should," David said. "I'm supposed to take it easy the day after a game."

"Okay," Cory said, and he seemed a little uncomfortable, as though he weren't sure what to do next.

Cory was a stocky boy, shorter than David, but big through the chest and middle. His hair was buzzed off this summer, which gave him a bullish sort of look.

"So what have you been doing?" David asked.

"Nothing. I'm getting bored already this summer. I want to go on a vacation when baseball is over, but my mom says we can't afford it." David knew that Cory's mother was divorced, and she didn't make a lot of money.

"We probably won't go anywhere either." But David didn't want to get into things like this. "Do you think anyone in the league will beat the Rangers?" he asked.

"I doubt anyone else can. But we will. You'll pitch against them next time. Brent is good enough to beat the other teams, and then you'll get the Rangers, and we'll win the championship."

"Paul watched the Rangers for a couple of innings the other night," David said. "They almost got beat by the Padres."

"Who's Paul?"

"Oh. That's what I call my dad."

"You call him by his first name?"

Cory had a way of saying everything in the same, rather flat tone. David didn't really know whether he was shocked or just mildly interested. And David wasn't sure he wanted to explain, but he said, "He's not actually my dad."

"How come you live with him?"

David hesitated. He thought about making something up. Or maybe just avoiding the subject somehow. But he couldn't think of any way to do that. And so he said, "My parents got killed."

"Both of them?"

"Yeah. We were in a wreck, and my dad and mom and brother all got killed. I was hurt pretty bad too."

Cory stared at him for a moment, and David hated the feeling. He wished he hadn't said anything. But then Cory said, "That's tough. Is Paul your relative or something?"

Cory's simple way of asking seemed to imply that he didn't think David was any sort of freak. But there were other things David still didn't want to say. "No. He was just willing to be my guardian."

Cory might have had more questions. But he had noticed the same thing David had. Lynn was walking toward them. "Hi, David," she said. She had on those baggy shorts. Her legs looked like a flamingo's—even the knobby knees.

"Hi," David said, mostly under his breath.

"Well, it surely is a lovely day," Lynn said, grinning, with her pink braces flashing. "And who is this nice young fellow?"

Cory looked over at David, as if to say, "What is this?"

David didn't say anything, but he rolled his eyes.

"Aren't you going to introduce me to your friend, David? Who knows? We might fall in love and get married. And we'll name our first child, a sweet little girl, after you."

David took a long breath, and then he said, "Cory, this is Pickle."

"Thanks a lot," Lynn said. And then she looked at Cory. "My name's Lynn. How do you like me so far?"

"You don't want to know," Cory said, but his voice

had taken on more life than usual, as though he thought she was funny.

"Well, I'm doing no better with you than I am with David. He doesn't like me—even though I caught for him the other day. If I had a mitt like that, I wouldn't have gotten a sore hand."

Now Cory was looking at David, obviously surprised.

David felt a need to save some face. "That's one thing she's pretty good at. She can catch. And she's got a good arm."

"So what's that supposed to mean?" Lynn asked. "'That's *one* thing she's good at.' You don't know how many talents I have. You don't know anything about me."

"I don't remember asking either," David said. It was not the sort of thing he normally said, and he had only done it now to keep up with her, in front of Cory. But David saw Lynn blink, saw the little head movement, and he knew he had stung her.

Still, she pretended she didn't care. "Well, I'll see you guys around. I've got better things to do than let you ogle my beauty all day." And she walked away, across the parking lot, but not so fast as the times before.

"Some beauty," David said.

"She's kind of cute," Cory said. "She's just too skinny."

The truth was, David thought she was sort of cute, too, although he had never exactly told himself that. She had a nice smile, even with the braces—and pretty green eyes. But that's not what he said. "She's kind of a pain."

"Yeah. I can see that." Cory was still watching as she

disappeared into the apartment building. But then he turned back and said, "Hey, who was that lady with your dad—or, your—"

"You can call him my dad."

"Anyway, who was that lady with him at the game last night?"

"Just a friend of ours."

"She was *gorgeous.*" Cory sat down on the grass, as though he planned to stay for a while. David hesitated, but then he also sat down. "How did your dad get to know her?"

"They used to work at the same place."

"Where?"

"Uh . . . at a hotel. The Jefferson Hotel downtown."

"What does he do?"

David didn't want to say this, but Cory seemed to be okay about everything. "He's a bellman."

"You mean like a bellhop?"

"They're called bellmen. In a nice hotel, they can make a lot of money."

"No kidding?"

"What did that woman do? Make beds?" He laughed.

"No. She was a cocktail waitress back then. In the lounge. It's not a dumpy little bar. It's a really classy place."

"I'll bet she got a lot of tips."

"But she's not some . . ." David couldn't think what to say. "She's about the nicest person I've ever known."

Cory shrugged, seemingly lost for anything to say about that, but David felt discovered, and he was embarrassed. "Look, I've got to go in now. Okay?" he said.

"All right. We could . . . hang out . . . or something."

"I can't today."

"Okay," Cory said, but David felt the awkwardness between them. For a second he almost decided to ask Cory to come inside with him. But he couldn't bring himself to do it.

"Well, I'll see you later," Cory said. He picked up his bike, and then he rode off. David couldn't tell whether he had hurt Cory's feelings or not.

At the next game, on Tuesday, David went out of his way to talk to Cory. He even told him to come over the next morning, and they could throw the ball around. David wasn't pitching that night, so he was fairly relaxed. His only worry was that Brent would mess up and lose to the Royals, who were not a very good team.

The game got off to a good start, though. David was playing third, and he made a great stop on a hard-hit ball, and then he gunned down the runner at first. He was a better pitcher than he was an infielder, so he loved it when he was able to help the team on a night he wasn't pitching.

In the bottom of the inning the Giants blasted the Royals' pitcher. David came up with runners on first and third. He hit a sharp ground ball up the middle that got between the shortstop and the second baseman. The runner on third scored.

When David stopped at first, he heard Paul yelling, "Way to go, David!" He glanced up to check, just on the off chance that Melissa had come again, but she wasn't sitting next to Paul.

Gabriel hit a shot to left field that skipped past the left fielder, and David ran hard, scoring all the way from first. By the time the inning was over the Giants were up, 6 to 0.

Brent had a little trouble getting the ball over the plate the next couple of innings, and he gave up three runs. But the Giants kept pounding the ball. At the end of three innings, the score was 11 to 3.

All the Giants' players were enjoying themselves. They were louder than usual, more obnoxious. They were really pouring the abuse on the poor Royals' pitcher—the third one by now.

When David was about to head back to the field at the start of the fourth inning, Coach McCallister called him and Joey and James back. He told three of the subs to take their places.

David didn't mind. He sat down on the bench and stuck his feet up against the fence, his cleats catching in the wire. James sat down next to him. "These guys stink," he said.

"They have some pretty good players," David said. "They just don't have any pitching."

Joey sat down next to James. He looked across James and said, "Not as good as you. Right?"

"I didn't say that."

James and Joey both laughed. "No. You just thought it," James said. James was the tallest guy on the team, and Joey was one of the smallest, so they looked a little funny alongside each other, but they were almost always together. Both of them had smart mouths. Maybe that was what they liked about each other.

"Hey, where's your girl tonight?" James asked.

David didn't answer. He wasn't going to get into all that again.

"I think she should come to all our games. She could be our cheerleader," Joey said.

"She has better things to do," David told him.

"Like what?"

"She's a college student."

"Cory told us she worked at a hotel—in the bar—where your dad's a bellhop." James grinned, as though the idea were funny to him. Joey laughed and then bent around to see David's reaction.

"He's a bellman."

"Isn't that a bellhop?" Joey asked, still laughing.

"It's not called that."

"Does he wear one of those little flat-top hats, like in the movies?" James asked.

"No, stupid. Haven't you ever stayed in a hotel?"

"Hey, don't call *me* stupid." James sat up straight. "I don't care what you *call* it—it's still the same thing."

"It's a good job," David said. He looked away. He didn't want to say anything more to these guys.

"I'll say this," James said. "I'd be a bellhop too if I could drop by the bar and meet girls like her."

"I'd wear *any* kind of hat," Joey said.

Both boys laughed hard, then James said, "I'd like to see her in one of those little cocktail waitress outfits."

"I'd like to see her *out* of one."

"Shut up." David stood up. "Just shut your mouths."

But James said, "Come on. We're just kidding around. Don't make such a big deal out of it."

David didn't know what to do. So he turned and walked to the end of the dugout and stood by the fence—in his usual spot. He wished he had never said anything to Cory.

David wanted the game to be over so that he could go home. Brent gave up another run, however, and the fourth inning seemed to last forever. All that time, James and Joey said nothing to David, but they laughed and talked in hushed tones, and David could only guess what they were saying.

By the time the inning was over, David was furious. Cory stopped outside the dugout and began taking off his chest protector. David walked to him, stood close, and said, "Keep your mouth shut about me from now on."

"What?"

"You know what I'm talking about. There's nothing wrong with my dad being a bellman. And Melissa's no slut."

"Hey, all I said was—"

David turned and walked back to his spot at the end of the dugout. He didn't say anything to anyone the rest of the game.

chapter 8

The Giants won easily, but David didn't say a word to anyone when the game was over. He avoided Cory—and James and Joey—and he slipped away. He met Paul coming out of the bleachers. "Let's go home," he said.

"What's wrong?" Paul asked.

"Nothing."

"Come on. You sound mad. What happened?"

David sensed that he'd better answer. He didn't want Paul to get upset. But he tried to keep it as simple as he could. "The guys saw Melissa the other night. Some of them were smarting off about her."

"What were they saying?"

"Just . . . you know. What a babe she was. You know the stuff boys say."

"She *is* beautiful, David. Guys are always going to notice that, no matter how old they are."

"I know. But they've got the wrong idea about her—because Cory told them she used to work in a bar."

"What if she did, David? Are you ashamed of that?"

"No. I just mean . . ." But David didn't know what he meant.

"David, most of the people I know work in bars or hotels. Does that bother you? Are you ashamed of what I do?"

"I didn't say that."

But now the silence returned, and David knew he had blown it. The truth was, he hated the idea that Paul carried people's luggage for them. He had watched how Paul acted around the customers—like he was a servant. How could he explain any of that to Paul, though?

"David, I'm no doctor or lawyer. But I make a decent living. And I didn't see any doctors or lawyers jumping in line to help you out when you had nowhere to go."

Paul was letting this build in his mind now, and David knew he had to say something to end it. "I'm sorry," he said. "I'm not ashamed of you. I didn't mean that."

It wasn't enough. David knew that. But what was he supposed to say?

Paul went back to his silence, and so did David. But David felt sick. Paul was so moody these days. Everything seemed to bother him. How long before he would blow it again?

The next morning David had just come in from pitching at his target when the phone rang. He answered and then felt his body stiffen when he heard a voice say, "David, this is Arnie."

"Hi," David said, but his throat pinched off so tightly that hardly anything came out.

"Remember the other day when you were in my office?"

"Yeah."

"I'm trying to think what I did with that report I was filling out. Did you happen to notice?"

"No."

"I thought I put it in your file. In fact, I'm almost sure I did. But it's not there now."

David clung to the phone. He wasn't going to chance any more words than he had to.

"Do you remember seeing me open the file cabinet—just before Paul and I left the office?"

"Yeah. I think so."

"Well, I don't know. The report isn't there, and it didn't fall between the files. I checked. Maybe I just made a mistake and filed it in the wrong place. I'll have to keep looking."

"Okay."

"David?"

"Yeah."

"I'm not accusing you or anything, but . . ." He hesitated and David heard how careful he was trying to be. "You told me to get rid of that file, and I told you I couldn't. You didn't decide to do that for me, did you? I mean, you didn't get in the file when I was gone?"

"No."

"David, I don't want to say this, but you sound nervous. Am I on to something here?"

"I'm not nervous. I just don't like to be accused of things I didn't do."

"Okay. I'm sorry about that." A long pause followed. "But, David, you didn't tell me the truth when I talked to you about Paul."

David could think of no excuse for that, and so, once again, he said nothing.

"David, I'm just trying to look out for you. I'll—"

"Arnie?"

"Yeah."

"What if Paul lost his job, or quit? What would happen?"

"Well, if Paul were out of work a short time, it wouldn't be that big of a deal. Long term, it could be a problem."

"Okay."

"Are you worried about something?"

"No. I just want to know how those things work."

Arnie ended with a request to call him if anything should go wrong. But David was trying to think what would happen if Paul got mad and quit. Would he be able to find another job?

When David hung up the phone, he sat down at the kitchen table. He was pretty sure Arnie hadn't believed him, and he felt rotten about all the lying. But what else could he do?

On Friday night the Giants played the Rockies. David was pitching again. Cory mumbled, "Hi," to David as they walked out to warm up before the game. David nodded in his direction, but he didn't say anything. David wanted to be left alone. He wanted to pitch a great game, and then he wanted to get away as soon as he could.

For two innings David was almost perfect. He was throwing the ball close to where he wanted it, every pitch. He struck out four of the six batters, and he got the other two on weak grounders. As he walked from the mound at the end of the second inning he heard Melissa shout, "Nice job, David! Keep it up." He hadn't known she was coming, but there she was, sitting by Paul, apparently having arrived a little late.

It suddenly occurred to him that he had a perfect game going—or at least started. It wasn't his perfect strikeout game, but he had retired the first six batters in order. Maybe he could pitch seven perfect innings. He walked to the end of the dugout. A couple of guys said, "Way to throw," and David knew he ought to talk to them. But he only said, "Thanks."

The guys were yelling, "Let's get something going!" And David knew that his team needed to score some runs, but it wasn't a huge concern. He was intent upon pitching a shutout, and he figured the Giants would get a few runs, sooner or later.

He looked up at the bleachers. Melissa was laughing and talking to Paul, looking happy and relaxed. He saw her tan legs stretched out over the seat in front of her, saw the way her hair flowed around her shoulders when she turned her head.

The Rockies' pitcher didn't have much speed, but he knew how to keep the ball low over the plate. All the Giants' batters were hacking down on the ball and hitting ground balls. Gabriel got on base on an error, but no one could bring him in.

In the bottom of the inning, David had no problem. The last three guys in the batting order came up, and David blew them away.

Brent started off the top of the fourth with a single up the middle, but Cory bounced one to short, and the shortstop took the lead runner at second. Then Chase rolled one to the first baseman, but that pushed Cory to second, in scoring position.

Now David had his chance. He could drive in the go-ahead run. But he chopped a grounder to third. The third baseman would have had a tough throw, and David might have made it, but Cory charged toward third. When the third baseman saw how far he had come, he turned and waited. Cory tried to retreat, but the third baseman threw back to the shortstop, who tagged Cory out.

Sometimes these guys just didn't think. David got tired of people doing stupid things like that. But he got his glove, and he told himself not to worry. He would just keep his string going.

He wanted three strikeouts this time. And he got the first one. The next batter was a big, strong kid. He took a wild swing at David's curveball and missed it. But David tried to put a little something extra on his fastball, and he got it up in the strike zone. The guy swung and lifted a fly ball to right field.

Joey took a couple of steps back and then realized that the ball wasn't hit as hard as he thought. He charged the ball, too late, and had to take it on one hop.

The runner really should have stopped at first, but he took Joey by surprise and raced on toward second.

And Joey panicked. He let fly with a throw that was over the shortstop's head. The Giants were just lucky that Dustin was backing up Chase.

The Rockies' runner got up and dusted himself off. He looked pleased with himself. His teammates were up and screaming now. "This pitcher ain't so tough," someone yelled. "We're getting to him now."

David was furious. The no-hitter was ruined—on a stupid mistake. Joey was such a lousy outfielder. But David was even angrier with himself. He needed strike-outs, not fly balls that his teammates could misjudge. And so he came hard with his fastball, and he really overpowered the next batter. The guy swung late on a couple of pitches low in the strike zone, and then he watched as a big curve bent over the plate.

Melissa was shouting again, "Way to go, David. These guys can't hit you."

David started the next guy with a fastball. The batter swung weakly, but he managed to tick the ball, and it dropped onto the grass and then spun toward the first-base line. David thought it was going foul, but he charged after it, just in case.

The ball seemed to stick, just inside the foul line. It was a good bunt, even if it was an accident. David got to it at the same time Cory did. But neither one had a chance to make a play, and the runner from second was already pulling into third.

"Tough luck," Cory said. "Don't worry. You'll get 'em."

David walked back to the mound, and he worked a good fastball in on the hands of the batter. The kid swung and popped the ball straight up. Cory flipped off his mask, moved under the ball and made the catch. Two outs.

But what an ugly inning. David needed another strikeout, just to feel that he was still in control. He reached back for something extra and fired a fastball that sailed high. When he took the throw from Cory, he heard the coach yell, "Don't force it, David." And he knew that was right.

The next pitch was perfect: good speed, on the outside part of the plate. But the batter reached out and arched a little fly ball to the right side. Joey charged again, but he had no chance to get to it.

The ball dropped in and the run scored. Now David's shutout was gone, and not one of these guys had actually stroked the ball. They had all gotten lucky. David kicked at the dirt. He couldn't believe this was happening to him.

chapter 9

David got the final out, but Jeff had to make a great play at second to stop a ground ball that might easily have gotten by him. David was glad the Rockies had only gotten the one run, but his confidence was shaken. As he walked toward the bench, the coach stopped him. "Ease off, David, and hit your spots—the way you usually do."

"Okay."

But the coach seemed to see his disappointment. "Hey, they got lucky. Don't worry. We'll get these guys."

"Yeah, I know," David said. But he hated the very idea that a couple of lucky breaks could make that much difference. It didn't seem fair.

All the same, the game kept going the same way. David didn't give up any more runs, but the Giants couldn't score. They were getting runners on base, but no one could get a clutch hit and bring any runs home.

As the Giants came up for their last time at bat, David was glad to get a shot to save the game. He stepped into the batter's box with one out and no one on base. He had to get something started and hope the other guys could come through.

David was patient, got a good pitch, and stroked the ball into left field for a single. That was a start. But Gabriel bounced a grounder toward the second baseman. David ran hard, hoping to beat the throw at second. Then he saw the shortstop stab to his left, backhanded, and saw the ball shoot past him.

David jumped up. He spotted the ball rolling into left field, and he took off for third. He stopped there and looked back. Gabriel, already on second, thrust his fist in the air and shouted, "All right, Brent. Bring us in."

David knew that Brent and Joey were not the best hitters on the team. But it wouldn't take much to get the game tied.

Brent seemed nervous, though. He stepped up to the plate and stood rigid, waiting. And on the first pitch, he swung hard and missed a pitch that was clearly low. The coach yelled to him to wait for a good pitch. But Brent swung again at the next pitch and bounced a grounder right back to the pitcher.

David broke from third, but the pitcher looked at him, and David had to retreat. The pitcher turned then and threw to first for the out.

The Giants were down to their last out. David yelled, "Joey, wait for a good pitch." And what he meant was, Try to get a walk. He knew Jeff, coming up next, was a much better hitter.

Joey showed no sign that he had listened to David,

but he did take the first pitch, and it was low. "Good eye!" David yelled. "Make him pitch to you." It was more than David had said during the whole game.

Joey laid off the next pitch, at his knees, but the ump called it a strike. The Rockies' defense was really talking it up now, and David could see how nervous Joey was.

The next pitch was low, but Joey went after it. He hit a grounder that rolled down the first base line. David ran hard, hoping the Rockies would mess the play up somehow. But the first baseman picked up the ball and then waited to tag Joey. David crossed the plate, but the game was over. He had lost 1 to 0. And suddenly, he was furious.

He spun toward Joey. "What did you swing for? That pitch was almost in the dirt."

"It was not," Joey shouted, and he ran toward David. For a moment, David thought Joey was going to throw a punch, but he stopped and yelled, directly into David's face, "Just shut up. You think you know everything."

David already knew he had done something stupid. But he wasn't going to apologize. He turned and walked away from Joey. By now, however, he saw that the coach was trotting toward him. "Come on, David, that's enough of that," he said.

David slipped by the coach and kept walking. He wanted to get away from everybody. At the dugout, however, Cory was waiting for him. "David," he said, "I'm sorry we didn't get you any runs, but you can't start blaming Joey."

"Leave me alone," David said, and he grabbed his

duffel bag. He heard someone say, behind him, "He doesn't care about the team. He just wants to get credit for a win."

"Maybe so," David said, out loud but to himself. "But at least I get my part done."

As David came around the fence, he saw Melissa coming toward him. He stopped in front of her, and she patted him softly on the shoulder. "Too bad, David. You pitched so well."

David nodded, but he didn't look at her.

"You shouldn't get mad though. Those guys did their best."

"Not really. Joey swung at a bad pitch." David tried to keep a level voice, but some of his anger spilled into the words.

Paul had come up behind Melissa now. "Come on, David," he said. "What kind of attitude is that?"

"Well, it's hard to lose such a close game," Melissa said. "Let's go drown our sorrows in a little ice cream."

David didn't really want to do that. He wanted to go home. But the three of them walked to the parking lot. Paul drove Melissa and David to the same hamburger place they had gone to the week before, and they sat in the same booth. But everything was different. Melissa didn't try to talk David out of his disappointment, but Paul was clearly upset. "David, don't make such a big thing out of this," he said. "I know it's hard to lose a game like that, but that's the way baseball is."

"You just had terrible luck tonight," Melissa said.

"It's not luck when guys don't *think* out there," David said.

Paul looked down at the table for a time, and when

he looked up, he seemed to be fighting against anger. "David, you are part of that team. You don't understand that. You stand at the end of the dugout away from everyone, and you never cheer for anyone. It's like the whole point of being there is only for yourself."

David wasn't going to have this conversation—especially not in front of Melissa. He sat stiff, staring straight ahead.

Finally Melissa said, "David's always been kind of quiet." She put her hand on Paul's arm. "Maybe he just doesn't like to make a lot of noise."

"No, Melissa. I'm quiet. But David is . . . something else. He won't connect with anyone."

David had been angry at Paul before, but never like this. He suddenly hated the man. Melissa shifted a little and put her arm around David, but he held stiff, wouldn't let her pull him close. What he thought of doing was getting up and taking off.

"Paul," Melissa said, "I think David has been through some hard things in his life—and it's had an effect on him. He's really a sweet kid." She gave David a little squeeze. "But some things are hard for him."

Paul nodded. "I know." He sat still for a moment, holding a cup of coffee with both hands. Most of the anger seemed gone, but not the disappointment, the sadness. But when David looked at Melissa, he saw nothing but love. She was the only one who accepted him completely.

Melissa put her hand on Paul's arm. At the same time, David finally let her pull him in closer. "I love both of you guys. I'm glad you're hanging in there together." No one said anything. Paul drank some of his coffee. David had forgotten all about his ice cream. "Paul, I'd like to talk to David alone for a minute, if I could," Melissa finally said.

"Sure," Paul said. He took his coffee with him, and he slipped out of the booth. "I'll wait in the car."

"We'll just be a minute," Melissa told him. And then, once Paul was gone, she slipped away from David a little, leaned toward him, and looked into his eyes. "David," she said, "what's going on? Are you okay?"

"Yeah. Sure."

"Don't do that, David. Talk to me."

"I just get mad when guys mess up. But I've got to quit being like that."

"David, I'm not talking about baseball. Why *do* you stand away from the other players?"

"When I'm pitching, I have to concentrate. I like to keep my mind on the game."

"Is that the real reason?"

"Yeah."

"Why don't you stay after the games and drink pop with the players, and celebrate?"

"I don't know. I just . . . don't like to. I'm not friends with any of those guys."

"Who *are* your friends, David?"

"I don't know. I know some guys at school. And sometimes I talk to a girl who lives in our apartments."

"Are they your friends?"

"Sort of." David had stopped looking into Melissa's eyes. He looked at the soft skin along her cheek and neck. And her hair, the way it touched her ear.

"Honey, you don't seem to trust people. Not even Paul."

David felt himself pulling away, even though he actually hadn't moved. He didn't like this. Why had she called him "honey"? It was something she would say to a little kid. And why was she only seeing Paul's side?

"What about his drinking?" David said, to defend himself.

"One slip, David, in a year and a half. That's not bad."

"He told me he wouldn't drink at all. If he does it again, Arnie will move me out."

"Is that what you're worried about?"

David tried not to show any emotion. "Yeah. Sure. Wouldn't you worry about that?"

"But that means you want to stay with him."

"Sure I do."

"Why?"

David shook his head a little, but he didn't answer. He was staring at the table, the gray surface.

"Why, David?"

"He's better than the other people I've been with."

"Oh, David, come on. Look what he's done for you."

"I know that."

"Do you appreciate it?"

"Sure." David began to slip along the seat toward the end of the booth. He wanted to go.

"David, you've got to listen to him when he tries to give you some guidance. He was right, you know, in what he told you just now."

"I know that."

"Well, show him you appreciate what he does for you. He needs that."

David took a long breath. He knew what she meant. But there were some things he just didn't know how to do.

That night, however, when David and Paul got back to their apartment, David did try a little harder. He told Paul he would make things right with Joey, and he admitted that he had to get to know all the players better. Paul accepted that, and he tried to chat a little. None of it seemed quite real, though. David knew he was mostly just saying what Paul wanted to hear. And Paul seemed to be going through the motions too.

When David went to bed that night, he was tired but not sleepy. He hated all the worry, all the fear. And so he slid back to his fantasy—the perfect game. In a game like that, luck was not important. The batters had no chance at all. And afterward, when he got home . . .

But he wouldn't let himself think about that. It wouldn't happen. It couldn't happen. He had to get his head straight about that.

chapter 10

Paul had to work an extra shift on Saturday morning. David was actually relieved that Paul wouldn't be home. He got up late and ate some cereal. Then he killed a little time watching an old movie. But he never got into it, and finally he decided to go out and throw some pitches even though he knew that once he did that he had nothing else to do all day.

His arm was stiff, but he kept throwing anyway. Then he saw Lynn coming toward him. "Hello, Pickle," David said. He had intended a little insult, but it wasn't in him this morning. The words came out so gently they almost sounded affectionate.

"Did you guys win last night?"

"No."

"*You* pitched, and you lost?"

David nodded.

"What happened?"

"We couldn't get any runs. We lost one to nothing."
He was tempted to put the blame on Joey, but he let it go.

"So how come you're being nice today? Just because your buddy isn't here?"

"I'm not being nice."

"Well, you're not being a jerk, anyway."

"I'm sorry. I'll do better next time."

Lynn grinned. "So do you want to eat clams with me?"

"What?"

"I'm going for a walk down to the docks, and I'm going to eat fried clams for lunch. Come on and go with me. I'll buy."

David was sure he didn't want to go. He just didn't know how to say it.

"Don't think up an excuse. Say no if you don't want to."

But that caught David off guard, and for some reason his reaction was to say, "I'll go."

"Really?" Her eyes brightened. "Okay, I've got to go get beautiful so you'll *gasp* when you see me. It'll take me ten minutes. Maybe fifteen. You won't change your mind while you're waiting, will you?"

David shrugged. "I don't think so," he said.

"Don't. You go do what you gotta do, or whatever, and I'll come by for you, at your apartment. Okay?"

She didn't wait for an answer. She took off running—and the girl showed some surprising speed. She charged across the parking lot and disappeared into the building.

David wasn't sure what to do, but he found himself wanting to take a quick shower. After, he decided to put on a pair of shorts and his favorite knit shirt. He was combing his hair, not quite ready, when he heard the doorbell ring.

When he opened the door, Lynn said, "Wow!" But David was probably more surprised. Lynn had on white pants and a green top that brought out the green of her eyes. She had brushed out her hair, too, so it was down over her shoulders. She actually looked pretty—for a pickle.

"You were supposed to gasp," she said.

"I did. Didn't you notice?"

"I was too busy gasping myself, I guess. David, you're so cute. You make my knees do weird stuff."

David could handle her smart mouth, but he didn't want this. He stepped out of the door so quickly he banged into her shoulder, and then he walked down the hall ahead of her.

"Okay, okay. I'm sorry," Lynn was saying from behind him. "I have this bad habit. I say whatever I think. My mom says I'm the weirdest person she knows."

David kept walking, but once outside, he let her lead the way. And she had the good sense to talk about something else. "I do this every Saturday," she told him. "I get clams at this little place on the docks. And then I wander around. I go to Farmers' Market, or I walk through stores, or I go over to Pioneer Square and watch all the street people."

"Isn't that a good day to be with your mom?"

"No. She just wants to rest. I drive her crazy."

David realized that if he talked about her family, she would ask about his, so he changed the subject. "Hey, you can really run," he said. "Have you ever gone out for track?"

"Yeah. This spring. But I quit after one practice."

"Why?"

"They make you run all the time."

"That's why it's called track."

"Well, it's *tiring.* Hey, do you want to do something fun?"

"What?"

"Just do what I do when we get to the overpass over the freeway." But the overpass was still half a block away. Now, strangely, she was the one who seemed to be changing the subject.

Lynn walked to the center of the overpass and then stopped. "Okay," she said, "look down." A steady stream of cars was moving underneath, the tires buzzing on the concrete. David wondered what she had in mind. He hoped she wasn't going to spit or drop rocks. Nothing would exactly surprise him.

A wire fence, above the concrete railing, kept them from being able to lean out, but Lynn stood tall and put her forehead against the wire, and then she looked down. David did the same.

"Okay, do you feel it?"

"What?"

"Just stare at the cars and see what happens."

David didn't know what she was talking about—and then the feeling hit him. He felt as though the cars were standing still and the overpass was flying forward. He pulled back.

"See, you felt it. Don't stop so fast. Just go for a ride." And then she mumbled, "Ooohhhhh, yes. Here I go."

David stayed with it a little longer this time. But he soon stepped back. He didn't like the sense that he was falling forward onto the freeway.

"Well, okay," Lynn said. "That's your first thrill for the day. No. Your second. Your first was when you looked at me after I fixed myself up, and you said to yourself, 'Hey, she looks pretty good.'"

"For a pickle," David said, smiling. It was somehow the nicest thing he had ever said to her—and they both knew it. She put her arm through his. But he didn't let that last long. He was already thinking he wanted to make this little excursion as short as possible.

"See that building over there—the tall one?" he asked.

"What? The Jefferson Hotel?"

"Yeah. That's where Paul works—I mean, my dad." David was really just trying to think of something else to talk about, but now he knew he had created a trap for himself.

"He's not really your dad, is he? Someone told my mom that. She finds out everything."

"Sounds like you do too."

The two of them had walked off the overpass and onto a sidewalk that descended into the heart of the city. Lynn had drifted a little farther away. Finally, she said, "David, you sure get mad a lot."

"I'm not mad."

"Oh. Sorry. You just sound mad. Look mad. Talk mad. But other than that, you're not mad."

"I just don't like people to talk about us. It's nobody's business."

David and Lynn stopped at a corner and waited for

a light. A truck was pulling across the intersection, revving its engine and discharging a black cloud of diesel smoke. Lynn waited for the noise to pass and then said, "People talk about me and my family too. And we've got a lot more to hide than you do."

The light changed, and the two of them stepped off the curb. "Like what?" David asked.

"Maybe I don't want to tell you."

"That's fine with me." But David really was curious.

"It's why my mom sends me to a therapist once a week, and it's why I'm so weird—according to my mother."

"You are pretty weird."

Lynn seemed to like that. She turned, in the middle of the intersection, reached up and ran her fingers through his hair. "I've been wanting to do that," she said. "I like your hair."

David walked away. He knew the people in the cars, waiting for the light to change, had to be watching them.

"Okay, okay," Lynn said. "I won't do any more stuff like that. And I'll tell you my big secret."

"You don't have to. I don't care."

"Yeah, you do." But then she didn't say it. She started walking faster for no apparent reason, or maybe because she could never keep the same pace for very long. "My dad's in prison," she said, suddenly. "He embezzled a bunch of money at the place where he used to work."

"Is this the truth or one of your old movies?"

"I'm sorry to say, it's the truth. Pretty strange, huh? You never knew a jailbird's daughter before, did you?"

David didn't answer. And Lynn dropped the whole matter.

But later, after she had led him to the docks and bought the clams, and then had picked out a little table by the water—and after she had eaten more than her share—she came back to the topic. "We used to be rich," she said. "Fairly rich, anyway. We lived in Bellevue in a giant house, and I was a little snob. Not as bad as my sister, but almost. And then last year—in November—the cops showed up at my dad's office and arrested him. Mom said it was a mistake, but it wasn't. And then it was like we were falling off a cliff—down and down and down."

"Did you lose your house?"

"We lost *everything*. They took it all to pay back the money my dad stole." Lynn looked toward the water. Some loose strands of hair blew across her forehead. "My mom has a good job now. And some things were in her name. So we get by. It's just that my life ended— and a new one started. And my dad, who was this nice guy with a lot of money, was suddenly a big crook." She looked back at David. "How am I supposed to deal with that?"

"I don't know. How do you?"

"Not very well. I tell myself I'm not my dad; I'm me. But when people ask me about him, I make up stuff." She looked toward the water again. A ferry was approaching, preparing to dock. Its wake was spreading and waves were slapping the piles under the dock. "I'm now like the world's champion escape artist." She hesitated. "And that, my friend, is how Lynn—a.k.a. Patty Pickle—got to be weird."

She was laughing, but David knew she wasn't doing well. And so he offered her something. "My whole life changed in one day, too," he said.

"I know. My mom told me about the car wreck, and your family. But how did you end up with Paul?"

David watched the rolling waves. "No one in my family could take me. Or at least no one would. So I got put into foster homes. And they kept moving me around. Finally I got sick of it, so I took off. I was on the streets for a couple of nights, but then I sneaked into the Jefferson Hotel, and Paul found me hiding by a Coke machine, trying to sleep."

"You mean, that's how you met Paul? And he ended up taking you as a foster child?"

"Yup."

"That's amazing. Paul must be some guy."

David nodded, but he hardly knew what to say about that. The whole thing was too complicated to explain.

"Your story is better than mine, David. You don't seem like the kind of guy who would run away."

"I was in a bad situation where I was," David said. "I couldn't stand it." But he let her believe that maybe the family was a mess. He didn't tell her that they just didn't like him.

"You seem okay now, though," Lynn told him. "You're not as messed up as I am."

"I wouldn't say that." But David knew he was treading on thin ice. He wasn't sure he should tell her any more.

"What do you mean?"

"I worry a lot."

"About what?"

"What's going to happen. I don't seem to have much to say about it."

"So who does?"

"Someday, I will."

Lynn let her hands move forward on the table, toward his arm, but not close enough to touch. "You'll be fine, David. You do things right. You do well in school and in baseball and everything."

"What about you?"

"I don't know. Now I'm supposed to start over in a new school where no one knows me. But I don't think kids are going to like me."

"A lot of them will. You know—if you're the way you are right now."

Lynn looked at him, steadily, for a long time. "But I can't be like this," she finally said.

"Why?"

"I don't know. It's like I'm not me anymore."

David nodded. "I feel like that sometimes too. Last night, I got mad at one of the players just because he swung at a bad pitch. I started yelling at him, like I was nuts."

"Well, that's good. Maybe you're not as weird as me, but at least you're not quite normal. I need a friend like that."

David laughed, and then he looked away. He didn't want her to think they would be hanging out together all the time.

"Don't tell anyone, okay?" Lynn said.

"What?"

"About my dad and everything."

It was the weakest thing she had ever said—and it took David by surprise. "I won't," he said. "Don't tell about me, either."

"David, you don't have anything to hide. Your parents got killed. That wasn't anyone's fault."

"I know. But don't tell about Paul not being my dad."

"Okay. I won't. Let's make a pact. Let's be blood brothers. We can cut our fingers and stick them together. Or better yet, we could forget about the blood, and just stick our lips together." She grinned, showing her pink braces.

David shook his head and then looked away, but he was smiling.

chapter 11

On Monday morning David was sitting on his balcony watching the mist burn away. He wanted the air to be a little warmer before he went outside to pitch. When the doorbell rang, he walked through the apartment and opened the door. Lynn was standing there in a huge, ratty T-shirt that hung almost to her knees. She was holding her baseball glove up for him to see. "Want to play catch?" she asked.

David had had fun with Lynn on Saturday. On their walk home she had thought of stupid things to do. David had found himself pulled along, even though Lynn embarrassed him. She had taken him into a department store, and she had tried on clothes. "So what do you think?" she would ask, and she would spin around. She knew exactly how to talk to the woman who was helping her. "I'll have to bring my mother down tomorrow," she would say. "I've got to get going on my school shopping before the summer gets away from me."

The sales clerk fussed over Lynn as though she were going to buy everything she tried on. And Lynn kept pushing the whole thing, trying on uglier stuff, striking poses, never laughing. And finally she even got David to try on a couple of jackets.

David knew he was in over his head. All this was funny, but it wasn't him. When they left the store, Lynn was hyper. She stopped to talk to a homeless guy who was holding up a sign that said, "Willing to work. Family hungry." She asked him all about his family, kidded with him about hoping he didn't really have to work for his money, and actually got him to laugh about that. David was standing back, cringing.

And yet, one side of David liked what was happening. It was so gutsy and confident. It was everything David was not—except maybe when he was out on the pitching mound.

But here she was now, first thing Monday morning, wanting to be with David again, and he didn't want her to start taking over his life. He didn't know how to tell her that, though, and so he got his glove.

He and Lynn walked out to the little strip of lawn, and he pitched, while she pretended to be his catcher—giving signals, chattering encouragement, even doing her own version of a radio announcer. And after her hand wore out, she watched him while he threw at his target. He wasn't letting loose with his hardest stuff, but he was picking his spots and hitting them, even calling them out to her. And she was impressed.

When he stopped, he found himself sitting down on the grass next to her, even though he had thought he was going to make an excuse and go inside. Lynn started asking him about the middle school. But he didn't know the answers to most of her questions. She wanted to know about the in crowd, and about the various social levels. David had never paid any attention to that sort of thing. He had gone to his classes, and he had gone home.

"So were the girls all after you last year?" she asked him.

"No."

"Look, David, I know they were interested. You probably just didn't pay any attention. Are you telling me that there's not one girl you like?"

David was about to say no, but then he said, on impulse, "Yeah, there is one, actually."

"That's what I figured," Lynn said. "What's her name?"

"I'm not saying." And then David realized his problem. She might think he was hinting around about her.

"What does she look like?"

"She's beautiful," David said. "She has blue eyes. Dark blue. And pretty hair—sort of blond, with lots of different shades in it. And she's . . . perfect. She's just the most perfect-looking girl I've ever seen."

"Wow. So tell me, what makes a girl perfect?"

David heard the tension in Lynn's voice. He knew what he was doing was cruel, so he backed off. "I don't know, exactly."

"I guess she's got a fantastic figure?"

"Well . . . yeah."

"Long legs. Cute fanny. Big boobs. I've got the picture."

"Not really. She's—you know—just right. She does have pretty legs."

Lynn tried to laugh. "Well, that's a new one on me," she said. "I thought the perfect girl had bony legs, red hair, and a zillion freckles."

David suddenly felt sorry for Lynn, and so he said, "This girl's not interested in me."

"She probably will be."

"Nope. Not ever. That's one thing I'm sure about." But David was surprised at the sadness those words cost him. And he knew that Lynn must have heard it in his voice.

The two sat for a time, looking away from each other, neither speaking, and then Lynn said, "Hey, listen, I've got to get going. My mom wants me to do some things for her today."

David nodded. "Okay," he said. When she got up, he thought of calling her back so he could explain. But the words didn't come, and she walked away. David felt like a jerk, but at the same time, he told himself it was just as well. He didn't want Lynn to think she was becoming his girlfriend, and he knew that's what she had been hinting around about.

David lay back on the grass and looked up at the thinning haze. And he thought of Melissa, not Lynn. He remembered the touch of her body when she had hugged him, the softness of her hair against his face. He wished that he could grow up suddenly. And he knew it was stupid.

He got up quickly and he turned to his target. He

rocked back and threw hard—way too hard—and wild-ly. The ball banged off the top of the wall and bound-ed past him. He turned and walked slowly back to it. He had planned to throw a few more pitches, but instead, he picked up the ball and walked back to his apart-ment.

There was no game scheduled on Tuesday, but on Thursday, David woke up knowing that he had baseball practice that day. He was really nervous about showing up for it. He wasn't mad about the last game anymore. He just felt stupid about what he had said to Joey, and he knew he ought to apologize. But that would mean bringing the subject up—and thinking of what to say. David couldn't picture himself going through all that. He hoped that if he let it drop the guys would forget about it.

The truth was, he sometimes wished he were friends with some of the players—or at least one of them. It would be nice to have someone to spend some time with. He could only pitch so long each day, and after, the days seemed to crawl by. But the idea of having a close friend—someone who came around a lot, called, wanted to do things all the time—frightened David. Friends seemed to want too much.

The day was very long, but David waited until the last minute before he walked over to the baseball field. He wanted to avoid the time when the guys were arriv-ing and acting smart, slugging each other and throwing insults around. He just wanted to practice and let them see that he wasn't mad. Maybe he could even talk to them a little more than usual.

As he walked toward the field, he could see that most of the players were already there. They were warming up, playing catch, and Brent was hitting fly balls to the outfielders. David saw Cory putting on his catching gear, so he decided to go over and say something to him. That would at least break the ice.

Cory glanced up and saw David, but then he looked away. "Hi," David said, but Cory didn't answer.

David didn't know whether Cory was still mad or whether he hadn't heard. So David sat down and changed his shoes. He stuck his street shoes in his duffel bag, and then he stuffed the bag under the bench. By then, Cory was walking toward home plate. David was about to head out to third base when the coach called out, "Hey, guys, come over here. Sit on the grass. I want to talk to you."

The players walked to the left-field side of the diamond, or trotted in from the outfield. They were wearing shorts and sweatshirts, or T-shirts, but not their uniforms. David wasn't sure how to let everyone know that he wasn't angry with them. The only thing he could think to do was to say hello.

And yet, every time he looked at any of the players, he noticed that their eyes snapped away. He knew that meant they were mad at him, and he wasn't surprised. He just didn't know what to do about it.

The coach talked about the game the team had lost. "Baseball is funny," he said. "On a certain day, any team can beat any other team. In the big leagues, the best teams win a hundred games or so, but that still means they lose sixty. When you lose one to nothing, you know that the slightest little thing could have made the difference. But teams that play smart and know the fundamentals are going to have the odds on their side."

He tucked his fingers inside his belt, and he looked around. "We were pressing too hard the other night. Everybody was trying to knock a home run when we needed to put a few singles together."

David was waiting. Sooner or later the coach would say it. But he talked about a lot of other things before he said, "And kids, let's not start getting on each other. I know it gets frustrating when we have a night like that. But if we start blaming each other, that only adds more pressure."

The coach didn't look at David, but a few guys did. David thought of raising his hand, thought of saying he was sorry about what he had done, but he couldn't bring himself to do it.

As the guys got up, after the coach's little speech, David looked over at Joey. He wanted at least to say hello to him. But Joey walked away.

And so David decided to wait for another chance. He walked out to the diamond to take some infield practice. He and Dustin always took turns at third base, but Dustin got to the base ahead of David, so he took the field first. He looked toward home plate and didn't say anything.

The coach was just getting set up. "All right, take one," the coach yelled, and he pointed at Dustin. Then he hit a sharp grounder to Dustin's left. Dustin took a couple of quick steps and scooped the ball up. He threw low to first, but James caught the ball on one hop.

"Nice pickup, Dustin," David said. It was the sort of

thing he usually didn't bother to say, but he figured that Dustin would know he was trying to apologize. Dustin, however, showed no sign that he had even heard.

"One more, and take a little more time on your throw, Dustin," the coach shouted. Dustin nodded. This time the coach hit a slow bouncer, and Dustin had to charge it. He took the ball on a high hop, set his feet, and made a good throw to first. "That's the way," the coach yelled.

And David said, "Good throw, Dustin."

Dustin walked off the field and let David take his position.

"Okay, David. Take one," Coach McCallister yelled. He hit the ball hard. It bounded straight at David, but it caught the edge of the infield grass, flattened out, and skidded under his glove. David spun around and chased after it. And somewhere, across the infield, he heard someone laugh.

David grabbed the ball and looped it back to the coach. As he glanced around, he saw all the infielders looking his way. And maybe it was his imagination, but they seemed pleased, as though they were glad he had made a bad play.

"Take another one, David," Coach McCallister shouted, and he hit the ball hard. David fielded this one fine, and he made a good throw. But no one said so. Not even Dustin, who was standing close by.

David knew by now that something was going on, maybe something planned, but he wasn't sure how to handle it. When the infield workout was over, the coach asked David to pitch for batting practice. And so he walked to the mound. Cory took up his position behind the plate. David threw some pitches to Gabriel, at bat, and no one said much of anything. But when Gabriel stepped out of the batter's box, and Jeff came up to the plate, David really wanted to break through all this. "I'm going to throw my beanball, Jeff," he yelled, and he laughed.

Jeff said nothing. He swung the bat a couple of times, and then got ready for the first pitch.

David had to know. He couldn't take this. He walked toward the plate. "Jeff, do you care if I throw a couple of curveballs, just to give you the practice?" he asked.

Jeff looked away.

David stood there for a moment. And then he said, "Cory, what's going on?"

Cory looked at Jeff. "So how's it going, Jeff?" he said. And Jeff laughed.

chapter 12

David didn't know what to do. Later, he wished that he had told the guys, right then, that he was sorry about what had happened at the last game. Instead, he stood for a moment, confused, and then he turned and walked back to the mound. He pitched batting practice without saying a word, and by then the players were going out of their way to make it obvious that they weren't going to talk to him.

When James swung and missed a pitch that was below his knees, he yelled, "Hey, keep 'em—" But he stopped and never finished his sentence. The infielders all laughed.

And it was at that moment that David told himself he didn't care. He didn't have to talk to these guys, and they didn't have to like him. He went about his business, silently, and when practice was over, he went home.

When he got home, he said nothing to Paul. He went to his room, and he lay on his bed. But by then, the resentment was gone, and what he felt was the numbness, the sense that he was still alone and always would be. The wall was still there, beige and empty, and he couldn't get past it. He didn't doubt for a second that this whole thing was his own fault, but he had no idea how he could change himself.

He soon slipped away from all that, however. He allowed himself some time to imagine himself in the big leagues, to let the vision take the place of the wall. He pictured the perfect pitches gliding from his fingers: batter after batter, swinging and missing.

When Paul stuck his head in the door, David was startled. "Hey, David, do you want to drive down and get a frozen yogurt?"

"Uh . . . no, thanks."

"Why not?"

"I don't know. I just . . . don't want one."

"Okay. I'm going anyway."

David suddenly realized the danger. He jumped up and chased after Paul. "I'll go," he said.

"That's all right," Paul said. "I think I'm just going to go for a drive. I need to get out of here for a while."

Paul didn't sound angry, but David was frightened about what this could mean. "Paul, please don't . . ."

"What? Drink?"

David didn't answer.

"That's what you think I'm going to do, don't you?"

"No, I just—"

Paul shut the door rather too firmly, going out. And worse, he was gone for a long time.

All evening David worried. He knew he should have gone with Paul, should have told him about the guys on the team and what was happening. It was the kind of thing maybe Paul could help him with, and Paul would have liked that. David didn't understand everything that was going on with Paul, but he was obviously struggling. If David had been willing to talk with him about his own problems, maybe Paul would have opened up too.

By the time eleven o'clock came, and Paul still wasn't back, David was frantic. If Paul was drunk, that might be the end of everything. David couldn't do anything about that. But maybe he could do something to take some pressure off Paul. He called the hotel and asked for Rob, who would just be starting the night shift.

"Rob, it's David," he said.

"Hey, how're you doing, Dave? How's the wife and kids?"

David was in no mood to kid around. "Has Ralph been bothering Paul a lot lately?"

"Yeah. You could say that. He gives Paul a hard time."

"Betty says he's trying to make Paul mad—so he'll quit."

"That could be right. I don't know."

"Could you tell the manager that?"

"What do you mean?"

"Just tell him what Ralph is doing. All the trouble he's causing. Maybe he'll make Ralph stop. Or fire him."

David heard the hesitation and his heart sank. "I don't know, David. Nobody likes Ralph, but he doesn't do anything that would get him fired. The only way that would happen is if the guests complained about him."

"Don't they ever do that?"

"Oh, a little, once in a while. You know, they don't like the way he hustles them all the time to sell them city bus tours. But no one has made a big deal out of it."

"He's making Paul mad all the time. I don't think he has a right to do that."

"I see where you're coming from, David. I could maybe make a comment to the boss, but I doubt it would do a lot of good."

"Okay."

"Hey, don't sound like that. I think Paul's handling it all right."

"Yeah. Okay. Thanks, Rob." And David hung up quickly. He had just heard a key in the front door.

David walked from the kitchen and looked at Paul as he stepped inside. Paul tried to smile. "Sorry I didn't come back sooner," he said. "But I didn't drink anything. I thought about it. But I didn't do it."

David was relieved. But something had to change. Paul was too close to the edge. David felt as though everything in his life was going wrong, and he had to do something, not just let things cave in on him.

When he went to bed, he tried to think of anything he could do. If he could make things okay for Paul, the problem with his baseball team really didn't matter so much. An idea had hit him when he was talking to Rob, but he wasn't sure it would work. He thought about it for a long time before he slipped out of bed and turned on his computer.

David stayed up late composing a letter to the hotel

manager—a complaint about Ralph. He said he had stayed at the hotel and the bell captain had constantly bothered him about buying city tours. "I've never met such a rude person," he wrote. "You need to get rid of him for the good of your hotel."

David liked that, but he didn't know how real it would look. He thought about a name and settled on William Johnson. He practiced it a couple of times—writing it as a loose scrawl, hard to read. And then he wrote it on the letter.

The next morning David found an envelope in Paul's room, and he looked up the hotel address. He knew he should send the letter from somewhere else, not Seattle, but he didn't know how to do that, so he walked to a post office a few blocks from the apartment, and he posted the letter.

Once the letter was gone, David wasn't as satisfied as he wanted to be. One letter probably wouldn't do a lot of good. And maybe the manager would figure out that it wasn't written by a hotel guest. But at least he had tried. Maybe he could wait a little while and then send another letter—and somehow figure out a way to get it sent from another state.

For the moment, however, David had another problem. The Giants were playing that night. He wouldn't be pitching, and that made things a little easier, but he didn't know how to deal with the players. He wished he could quit the team, but he couldn't let go of baseball.

That evening at the ballpark, David split off from Paul and walked toward the players, who were warming up. Gabriel almost said hello before he caught himself. Instead, he turned and said something to Brent.

David felt jittery. He knelt down and changed his shoes, and he stuffed his sneakers in his duffel bag. He decided to stick his bag in the dugout, and then to go about things the way he always did. But when he stood up, he saw Melissa walking toward him. Some guy was with her. He was big, with huge shoulders and a thick neck, like a football player.

David walked toward Melissa, so that he could get some distance between himself and the other players. "Hi, David," she called to him. Then she waited until they walked closer to each other before she said, "I want you to meet my friend John."

David nodded. John reached out and shook David's hand. Then he put his arm around Melissa's shoulder. David was stunned. Melissa had never mentioned this guy. He was handsome, in a way, but he was like a cartoon character—exaggerated. His jaw and chin were too big and square, his eyebrows too heavy.

"Melissa told me all about you," John said, in a voice that was not as deep as David expected. "She says you're quite a pitcher."

"I'm not pitching tonight," David said.

"You play third base when you're not pitching. Right?"

"Yeah. But I'm a better pitcher than I am an infielder."

"Well, it should be fun to watch, anyway. I haven't been to a Little League game for years."

"It's Pony League," David said, becoming irritated with this guy's style. "Little League is for young kids."

"Oh, yeah. I guess that's right. You're big guys, aren't you?" He grinned.

"John had a scholarship to play college football," Melissa said. "But he wanted to concentrate on his studies."

"I knew I wasn't going to make it to the pros," John said, "so I figured it was time to get serious about school. But the UW did recruit me pretty hard."

Why did these two think David was interested in any of that? Melissa was acting stupid, leaning on this guy, bragging about him, acting like he was some big deal.

Paul had spotted all this, and he came down from the bleachers, and then the introduction and the discussion about John had to start again. "John's studying business," she told Paul. "He wants to open up a company of his own, eventually."

"Yeah, I may have to work for someone for a while. And put a little money away. But in the long run, I want to be my own boss."

David didn't trust him. He was way too impressed with himself. He was wearing a white knit shirt that stretched over his chest muscles, like he wanted to show off his build. But the worst was that he wouldn't take his hands off Melissa.

David saw what was happening to Paul. He was being nice, taking on that bellman style of his, talking softly, but at the same time, he was withdrawing. David saw his eyes run to Melissa, ask for something, and then look away. He seemed old and out of date.

David went out to warm up. Paul and Melissa and John climbed into the bleachers and sat together. But when David glanced up at them, it seemed as though John were taking up all the space, and Paul had somehow shriveled almost to nothing.

When the game started, David had trouble concentrating. He was relieved that no one hit the ball in his direction, and relieved that Brent was getting the ball over the plate. But more than anything, he just wanted this game to be over as fast as possible.

Once the Tigers had gone out in order, David trotted across the diamond to the dugout on the first-base side. That's when he noticed Lynn sitting on the front row of the bleachers, near the dugout. She clapped her hands and yelled, "Good job," even though David hadn't done anything.

David nodded at her, and then walked into the dugout and all the way to the end. He hated the tension, the eyes glancing toward him, the whispering. But all that was nothing compared to that big idiot up in the bleachers with his arm around Melissa.

David watched Melissa talk to the guy, with her face close to his. She was hardly watching the game. Suddenly David hated her. She was stupid. If she didn't know that guy was a jerk, then she deserved him.

Jeff led off, and he hit a line drive just inside first base. He went in to second standing up, rounded the bag, and bluffed a move to third, but the coach held him up. All the guys on the bench cheered. But David wasn't part of that. He said nothing.

The Tigers' pitcher seemed to let Jeff's opening shot shake him. He walked both James and Dustin, and Cory, the clean-up hitter, came up with the bases loaded and nobody out.

David was batting fifth, so he walked out to the on-deck circle. He hoped Cory would walk, so the bases would still be full. He wanted to knock one over the fence, something he had only done once this year. He wanted to do it with John watching.

Cory took a pitch inside, and the players all yelled, "Good eye, Cory." Cory took another pitch, down low, and the Giants' bench got all over the pitcher. "You can't throw strikes and you know it, kid," Joey was shouting.

Cory swung at the next pitch and lifted a high fly to short left field. The shortstop drifted back, but the left fielder charged ahead, called for the ball, and took it. Jeff bluffed a move after he tagged, but he held up when the left fielder made a good throw to the plate.

One away. Bases still loaded.

And suddenly the team became silent. Some of the parents shouted, "Drive 'em in, David," but the players said nothing.

The quiet stabbed at David, no matter what he tried to tell himself. He saw the coach, on the third-base side, look toward the dugout. "Let's keep it going, David," he said as he clapped his hands, but he was looking at his players, obviously confused by what was happening.

David heard Paul yell, "Just meet the ball, David," but not with his usual intensity. And when David heard a female voice shouting loudly, he realized it was Lynn's, not Melissa's.

David got set in the batter's box. He tried to be angry. He told himself he was going to hit a shot so far over the fence that his teammates would have to cheer. But the words didn't penetrate. He felt weak.

The pitcher took his sign, nodded, and then checked the bases. He pitched from the stretch position, and fired a pretty good fastball. David saw the ball well, but he swung way too hard, and missed.

He stepped out of the batter's box. His coach yelled, "Come on, David. Just poke one somewhere."

Paul was yelling the same thing. And so was Lynn. "Don't try to kill it, David," he heard her say.

But the bench was silent.

David had to show those guys. And John. He got set and waited. But he swung as hard as before, reaching awkwardly. And again he missed.

David talked to himself. "Don't be stupid. Get yourself under control. Stand in there and take a good swing." He took a deep breath. The pitch was outside, and he was ready to trigger, but he held up.

The next pitch was high. Now the count was two and two, and the pitcher would be nervous about going to a full count. He might tend to let up a little, and aim.

David was right. The pitch was over the plate and fat. And David was ready. He met the ball, solid, and it jumped off his bat and shot toward the gap in right center. For a moment David thought the center fielder might run it down, but it was hit way too hard. The ball got past the guy and rolled to the fence. David wheeled into second with a stand-up double, and three runs scored.

When David stepped on the bag at second, he turned, quickly, and looked back at the players. They had charged out of the dugout, and they were slapping hands with the guys who had just scored. But no one yelled to David.

So David looked at the bleachers. He saw Paul and Melissa and John, all standing up, cheering and clapping. But then Melissa turned to John, and she seemed to be terribly interested in something he had to say.

chapter 13

The Giants, as it turned out, had an easy night of it. They scored runs easily, and Brent pitched his best game of the year. David got another hit before he left the game, and he made a good catch on a line drive, at third. In fact, he played his best defensive game of the season. The Tigers got three runs, mostly on errors when the bench players were in the game, but the Giants won, 12 to 3.

And yet, none of it mattered to David.

No one on the team ever spoke to him. And once the game was out of reach, and they were having a good time in the dugout, the mind game turned uglier. In the final inning, when Joey was coming up to bat, Jeff yelled, "Don't swing at any bad pitches, Joey. You know how that upsets *some people.*"

Joey laughed, and so did a lot of the other players.

But David didn't move. He just held his ground and pretended not to hear.

When the game was over, David grabbed his duffel bag and walked around the fence. Melissa was walking toward him. "David, honey, we have to go. But I just wanted to tell you what a great job you did." She stopped in front of him and gave him a quick little hug, with a couple of pats on the back.

David stepped away, and then he nodded.

"John says you're really going to be good. He wants to come back and see you pitch." David nodded. Then Melissa hurried back to John, who had been waiting, and they both waved.

Paul was walking toward David now. "Good game," he said, but David could see no life in his eyes.

Paul said very little on the way home. He didn't try to pretend that things were all right. David thought Paul might ask what was going on, why the guys wouldn't cheer for him, but he obviously didn't want to talk, and that was okay with David.

When the two got back to the apartment, Paul opened the door for David and then said, "I just remembered, I need some cigarettes. I'll be back in a few minutes."

"Okay," David said, and he told himself not to worry. Paul hadn't gotten drunk the night before when he had taken off. So David took a shower, and then he sat on the balcony and waited. For the first half hour he assumed that Paul really had only gone for cigarettes. After an hour, however, he began to get scared. He thought about the way Paul's eyes had looked.

It was getting cool, but David sat outside in his

shorts and a light T-shirt, and he watched the lights on the ferry boats that were crossing Puget Sound to Bainbridge Island. Slowly, he let the numbness creep inside him. Eventually, he walked inside. But he didn't turn on the TV, didn't try to read. He just sat on the couch and waited. Another hour went by, very slowly. And then another.

David didn't go to bed, but he eventually lay back and drifted off to sleep on the couch. He woke up in the middle of the night, cold and disoriented, and he decided to get into bed. He checked Paul's room, on the off chance that he had come in and not noticed David on the couch, but Paul was not there.

David slept for a while, but he woke up early. He got up quickly and checked Paul's bedroom. Paul had still not come in. David didn't know what to do. He thought of calling Melissa, but he wasn't sure he wanted to see her right now. And there was nothing she could do. He thought of calling hospitals, too, or the police. But he kept hoping that at any minute the door would open. Even if Paul had gotten drunk, Arnie didn't have to know.

The morning passed slowly. It was gloomy outside, and a light drizzle was falling. It was almost ten o'clock when David finally thought to eat some cereal. He wasn't hungry, but he was so anxious and worried that he was happy to think of something to occupy a little time. He was sitting at the kitchen table when the doorbell rang.

David's heart began to beat hard as he walked to the door. He half expected to find a policeman there. But it was Lynn, with a jacket on. "So, big hero, do you want to take a walk in the rain with me—and eat clams for lunch?"

"I can't." He held on to the door, only half open.

"Why not?" She stepped closer, leaned against the door frame, and grinned. She was wearing a baseball cap, with a pony tail sticking out the back.

"I just can't. Not right now."

"Is this the old treat-her-rotten-and-she'll-go-away game?"

"No. I just . . ." But he didn't want to tell her what was going on.

"Look, David, I'm sorry. I stayed away for two days, and I thought you might call me, or come up and ask me to catch for you. But you didn't. So I went to your game, like an idiot, and you left without saying a word to me. Every now and then, you treat me like you sort of like me, but obviously you don't. And I like you so much that it makes me do all these stupid things. But I won't anymore. I'll leave you alone."

"I . . . uh . . . like you all right."

She rolled her eyes, and then she turned to walk away. But she suddenly turned back. "David, you are *so* stupid," she said, in that husky voice of hers.

David shrugged. He didn't know exactly what she meant, and yet, the accusation seemed right.

"I saw her last night."

"Who?"

"You know who."

"Melissa?"

"I don't know what her name is. But I know she's the *girl* you were talking about. Except she's no girl. She's got to be twice your age."

David looked past Lynn, not at her.

"She's gorgeous, David. Perfect. Just like you said. Every man in the place was staring at her."

"She's just my friend, Lynn. She used to work at the hotel where Paul works."

"And you're in love with her. Hey, I know all about it. I was in love with this guy who worked at the 7-11 over by our house in Bellevue. I used to imagine his wife dying of cancer, and him turning to me for comfort."

David still wouldn't look at her.

"It's stupid, David. You go ahead and live in your dream world." She reached out and pushed the door open a little wider. "But I'm going to be a knockout someday, and you're going to hate yourself for passing up your chance."

David began to put a little pressure on the door and she dropped her hand. "But I'm not good enough yet. Is that the idea?"

David stood for a time, taking the question seriously. And then he said, "Pickle, I'm a mess right now. I don't know what I think . . . about anything."

"You don't have any friends, David. And you don't want any. Cory told me what's going on with the team. I could be the best friend you ever had, if you would just figure that out."

David sort of knew that. But he didn't tell her so.

"Well, see you around," Lynn said. "I won't bother you anymore." She took three or four steps away, and then she stopped and looked back. David was still standing at the door. "Dave, my boy, do I have to tell you everything? When I walk away, you're supposed to say, 'Oh, Lynn, don't leave me. I want you in my life.'"

David tried to think what to say.

"Never mind. David, I'm the stupidest person in the universe. I swear. I don't know why I say stuff like that." And this time she walked away fast. She was really leaving.

David, in that instant, saw a sudden image of the empty day ahead of him, and he said, "Wait a sec."

Lynn was well down the hallway, but she spun around, looking shocked. And for once she didn't speak. She just waited.

David stepped into the hall. "Paul took off last night," he said. "And he hasn't come back. He used to drink a lot, and I'm afraid that's what he's doing now. Or maybe he's gotten hurt. I don't know."

"Oh, man," she said, and she slowly walked back. "And then I show up, smarting off, as usual."

"That's okay. I just don't know what to do right now."

"I can hang around with you, if you want."

"Yeah. That might be good."

She nodded, and stood there for a moment, but then she came inside.

David finished his breakfast, and then he and Lynn sat on the balcony. And they talked—mostly about where Paul might be and what might happen to David if Social Services found out. When the phone rang, it was Melissa. David told her what was going on, and she didn't seem all that surprised. "I could tell how unhappy he was last night," she said. "That's why I called." She told David that she had to get to her classes, but that she would come over later that afternoon.

When David returned to the balcony, Lynn was standing at the rail, looking out toward Elliott Bay. The rain was a little heavier now, and the water in the bay was a solemn gray.

"That was Melissa," David said.

"I know. I heard what you told her." Lynn sat down on a rickety old lawn chair, facing David, who had just sat down himself. There was a little glass table between them. "Was I right about what I said? Is Melissa the girl you told me about?"

David looked at Lynn, watched for any sign that she was teasing, but he didn't find it. And so he nodded. And when she didn't comment, he added, "But I know it's stupid."

"Of course. You always know stuff like that is stupid. But it doesn't change how you feel." Lynn looked down at the table. "If I looked like her, I'd stand around all day and just gaze at myself in the mirror."

"You said you're going to look great."

"And you bought that?"

"Didn't you mean it?"

Lynn looked out across the city again. "David, I just talk. I never know what I really think. Mom tells me I'm going to be pretty, and I want to believe it. But all I can see is what I look like right now."

David couldn't really picture Lynn as gorgeous, maybe ever. But he had never been able to talk to anyone the way he could talk to her. He liked that she knew about Paul, and about David's past, and the way that nothing like that seemed to bother her.

"So what's the deal with you and the team?" Lynn asked.

"Those guys all hate me."

"Cory said it's your fault. He said you won't talk to anyone—except to chew guys out if they mess up."

David found himself slipping inside himself. "I only got mad once. The rest of the time, I just like to keep my mind on my pitching."

"Come on, David. You could be friends with those guys. You don't want to."

"I started to be friends with Cory, and then he blabbed all kinds of stuff about me to the other guys on the team."

David could feel Lynn looking at him. He looked at her hands, resting on the table, and all the freckles, even on her fingers. He thought of Melissa's pretty hands.

"There's more to it than that, David. You push people away."

David didn't want to talk about this.

"All I'm saying is—"

"Don't, okay? I'm worried about Paul right now. That's all I can think about."

"Okay. Fair enough." But then she asked, "What happened last night? Why did he take off?"

"I don't know. He's not very happy. And then Melissa brought this guy to the game with her. I think that really bothered him."

"Why?"

"I think he keeps hoping that she's . . . you know . . . interested in him."

"My gosh! This is some woman. Paul's too old for her, and you're too young. And she's got both of you in love with her."

David had never seen the stupidity of it quite so clearly. But he felt sorrier for Paul than he ever had before. He wondered where he was, what he was going through. "Paul's had a lot of rotten things happen to him too," David said. "I think he wishes he could live his life over."

Lynn tugged at her baseball cap. "You really like Paul, don't you?"

"Yeah. Sure."

"But I guess you wish you could have your own dad back."

For quite some time David didn't say anything. He thought of telling Lynn some things that he had never told anyone. But he couldn't do that. Instead, he said, "I can't stand sitting here. Do you want to go with me to look for Paul?"

"Sure," Lynn said.

chapter 14

David and Lynn walked downtown to the hotel. David was nervous that Paul might have come in and cleared out his locker. Maybe he was headed back to San Francisco. David didn't want to say much to anyone, but he thought he could find an excuse to get into the bellman's room and check. The only problem was, when he and Lynn walked into the lobby of the hotel, the first person they saw was Ralph, who was sitting near the doorway at the bellman's station.

"Hey, kid," he said. "What did you do, find yourself a woman?"

David ignored that. "Hi," he said. But he was thrown by this situation. He had hoped to get a key to the bellman's room from the desk clerk, and not have to face Ralph.

"Paul doesn't work today," Ralph said. "You ought

to know that." He took a draw on a cigarette and then blew the smoke in David's direction.

"I know. But did he stop by this morning? He said . . . he might do that."

"I haven't seen him. But I was busy until just a little while ago."

"Could I get in the bellman's room for just a minute?"

"What for?"

"He was going to pick something up—from his locker. If he didn't get it, I will."

"What was it?"

David hesitated. "It was just . . . something he wanted. Could I look?"

"Hey, you just want to get this little redheaded girl in the back room and feel her up. I know how you kids are." Ralph dropped his head and covered his mouth, and he laughed.

"Could I just—"

"No way. If Paul needs something, he can come by himself. I don't let anybody in that room."

David knew better than to mess with Ralph. He walked to the front desk. Lynn followed. He stepped up to Harold and said, "You haven't seen Paul, have you?"

"No. Not this morning." Harold was older, with thin white hair and eyes that were yellowed around the edges, like old paper. He looked at Lynn, as though he wondered who she was.

"Hi," she said.

David realized he would have to reveal too much if

he asked anything else. "Okay," he said, and he turned to walk away.

But just then Ralph came around the corner. "Say, Ralph," Harold said. "Have you seen Paul this morning?"

Ralph looked at David. "No, I haven't. What did he do, kid? Take off on you?"

"No."

"Well, he will. Sooner or later."

David took a step away, but then he stopped. "Why do you do that? Why are you always on his back?"

Ralph waved his hand, as if to brush the words aside. "You don't know what you're talking about, kid."

"Just leave him alone," David said. "You're always . . ." But David suddenly felt his throat catch, and he knew he had to get away from this guy. He headed for the front doors.

"You might want to look for him over on Pike Street," Ralph called after David. "He's probably flat on his face in some dive over there. Or he's shacked up with some old lady over at that dump of a hotel where he used to live."

David was furious. He walked hard, with Lynn hurrying to keep up. "What a total loser," she was saying.

David couldn't talk. He kept walking. And he realized that he was heading for Pike Street. He *was* going to ask about Paul at the hotel where he had lived at one time. David had thought of that before, and unfortunately, he knew Ralph's suggestion had some logic in it.

Lynn followed David into the old hotel, but she seemed stunned by what she saw. "What's this, David? He wouldn't be in here." The smell of the place, the dust and the stale smoke, was disgusting. Near the door, in the lobby, was a tattered old sofa, as shabby as the worn-out carpet.

"You can wait here," was all David said, but Lynn followed him to the front desk.

"Do you know Paul Lambert?" David asked the man at the desk.

A heavy man with thick glasses glanced up from a newspaper that was spread before him on the desk. "Sure," he said.

"Have you seen him?"

"Who's asking?"

"I'm his . . . son. Have you seen him?"

"He don't have a son."

"I'm actually his foster child. Do you know about that?"

The man nodded. And then he said, slowly, "I haven't seen him. But he checked in last night. The night clerk said he came in drunker than a skunk. Could hardly walk. I'm sure he's sleeping it off."

"What room?"

The man thought for a moment. "Let me call the room and see if he answers. He may not want anyone up there yet."

The man stepped into a little back room. Lynn put her hand on David's shoulder. "Are you okay?" she asked.

David was breathing hard. He was trying to think. "At least we found him," he said. But he had no idea what was coming next. It was probably the beginning of the end.

The clerk was gone a minute or so. When he reappeared, he looked solemn. "I woke him up, and he don't sound good," he said. "He wasn't too excited about you coming up. But he said he guessed it was all right. Room four-oh-six." The man pointed to an elevator.

"Thanks," David said.

When Lynn followed David toward the elevator, the man called, "I didn't say anything about the girl. I doubt he wants her coming in there."

"Maybe you better wait down here," David said.

Lynn glanced around. "It's kind of creepy," she said.

"Okay. Come up. But I don't know what Paul will say."

"David." He stared at her. "I just really want to help. Some way or another."

David nodded, and pushed the button for the elevator. Then the two rode to the fourth floor and found their way down the dark hallway to room 406. And David knocked. When the door finally opened, Paul was standing there in wrinkled gray slacks and an undershirt. His belt wasn't buckled. His hair was all over, and he needed a shave, but what struck David most was the pale yellow of his skin.

Lynn stayed back a little, but Paul saw her immediately. And David saw the surprise in his eyes.

"Paul, this is my friend from the apartments. She helped me look for you."

Paul nodded, looking destroyed—humiliated. But he stepped aside and let the two come in. The room was repulsive, the smell of smoke and sweat powerful in the dark air. Paul walked over and sat down on the rumpled bed. He still hadn't said a word. He reached for a pack of cigarettes but then set it back down. "I guess you don't need any more smoke," he said, softly to Lynn, politely.

"Let's go home," David said.

Paul had been looking at the floor, or at his bare feet, but his head came up slowly. "I can't do it anymore," he said. "I tried, David. But I just can't. You need to call Arnie and get placed with a decent family."

"That's not what will happen, Paul. You know that. They'll dump me in some facility for a while, and then stick me with somebody who gets paid to take in kids."

Paul didn't answer for a time. He was looking down again, his elbows on his knees. Lynn was standing at the door with her back pressed against it. "I think you'll still be better off," Paul said. "I lasted as long as I could."

"Is this about Melissa?"

Paul looked up again. He let out a gust of breath. "I guess I'm not that hard to figure out," he said. And then, after a moment, "But there's more to it than that. I'm not a father. I've tried my best, but I just don't know how to do it right."

A long silence followed. David knew there were things Paul wanted. But the closest he could come was to say, "Paul, I've been very worried. I was afraid something had happened to you."

Paul stared at him. "You knew what happened. I just did what you expected me to do again and I went all the way this time."

"Come on, Paul," David said. "Nothing's happened. No one knows. We can go home. I won't say anything to Arnie."

"And then you'll wait for it to happen again."

"It doesn't have to happen. You can pick up where you left off . . . and do better this time."

"And see Melissa with that *John* guy? Go back to the

hotel and face *Ralph* every day? Then come home and *pretend* I'm a father? You don't respect me, David. You don't listen to me. I guess I can't blame you for that, but I can't keep it up. I've got to get out of all this—and get away from this town."

"And David gets dumped," Lynn said.

Paul was taken by surprise. He looked at Lynn.

"I thought you were a grown-up," Lynn said, "but you're not. You're just like my dad."

"Come on, Paul!" David shouted. "Quit feeling so sorry for yourself. You've made *promises* to me. You can't just walk away from them."

But Paul didn't respond. He was looking at the floor again.

David knew he had to back off. He couldn't lose his temper right now and blow the top off everything. He had to think of some way to salvage things, to smooth things over. "Paul," he said, "I understand about Melissa. That's just the way it is. There's nothing you can do about it. But you like the hotel, except for Ralph. And sooner or later Ralph will get himself fired. Then the hotel won't be so bad."

When Paul didn't say anything, David looked for something stronger. "I don't think Ralph is going to last much longer. Wouldn't things be all right if he weren't there?"

"Why would Ralph get fired?"

"People are complaining. The manager got a letter about him."

"When?"

"This week."

"How do you know?"

David was caught in a corner. "I just do. Rob told me. He told me people complain about Ralph all the time."

"David, why do you lie? You haven't talked to Rob."

"I *did*. I called him the other night. So don't call me a liar." And now the anger was back, beyond David's control. "The only time I lie is when I have to lie for *you*."

"No! You don't have to do that. I'll look out for myself."

"But you don't. I have to cover for you."

Paul stood up and pointed a finger at David. "The only time you covered for me was when you lied to Arnie. And I told you not to do that."

"That's not the only time."

"Name another one, then."

"I stole that report that Arnie wrote on you. And I lied to Arnie about doing it. And I've . . . done other things." But David's anger had begun to melt.

"Stole the report? How?"

"It doesn't matter."

"David, that's nuts. What other things have you done?"

But David wasn't going to say. He didn't want to bring up the letter. It seemed so stupid now.

"I'm not going to let everyone run my life. I'm not going to give up, like you."

"David, you're nuts. You're thirteen, and you think you can control everything."

"Someone has to have some control, Paul. No one *wants* me. And no one is going to take care of me. I have to do that for myself." David felt the tears coming, but he didn't want to cry.

"No, David." Paul pointed his finger again. "You won't *let* anybody take care of you."

"What good does it do? Everyone just pulls out on me. Or they dump me off on someone else." And now David was crying, no matter how hard he tried not to.

Paul was silent for a time. And then he said, softly, "Look, David, I know it was tough to lose your family. I know you miss having your own dad, but I—"

"No! I don't."

"What?"

"I don't miss him." Time seemed to stop. David could see a new reality in front of him and he hardly knew how to deal with it. And yet, he had been dealing with it for such a long time.

"David, why would you say something like that?" Paul's voice had softened.

"My dad used to drink too. I hated him for doing that."

"What difference does that make now?"

Something seemed to come apart inside David. "He'd get drunk and cause trouble with the neighbors. And then he'd make me lie about it to the police. And he drove too fast. He killed my mom—and my brother—driving like that in the rain. And drinking beer. I hate him." David gulped, hung on for a moment, and then he shouted the words with all his force. "I hate him! I hate him! I hate him!"

"Oh, man." Paul stepped over to David, took him in his arms. "No wonder we're so much alike," he said.

David clung to Paul, his face against his chest, and he sobbed.

chapter 15

Paul got his shirt and shoes on after that, and he and David and Lynn drove home. When they got out of the car, Lynn said, "I'll take off."

"Okay. I'll see you later," David said.

She looked at Paul. "I had no business saying what I did. I always talk too much."

"It's okay," Paul said. "I had it coming. Come and see us sometime." David took that to mean that Paul wasn't going anywhere.

As soon as Paul opened the door to the apartment, he said, "Sit down, okay?"

David sat on the couch, and Paul got a kitchen chair, so he could sit close, facing David. "I feel like I need to explain some things, David. I've been thinking about everything on the way over here."

"Okay." David knew this was a good sign, but it still made him nervous.

"I've had some things on my mind lately. I'm finally realizing how much I've messed up my life—and that it's too late to do anything about it."

"Why is it too late?"

Paul thought about that. "When Arnie let you come live with me, I had it in my head that I was going to do something right for once. But I messed up being a father before, and I'm no better at it this time around."

"A lot of that is my fault, Paul."

"No. I've been trying to push it off on you. But you're thirteen. And you've been through a bunch of stuff in your life, more than I'd imagined. You're not supposed to have things figured out. I am."

"Maybe no one has things figured out."

Paul smiled. He folded his arms and looked down. "Maybe not. But I see what's coming. If we stick this out together, you'll leave in a few years. And then . . . I can't think what I'm going to look forward to. All my life I've burned my bridges, cut myself off from the people I'd like to have close to me now."

"Paul, I'll . . . keep in touch. We'll always be friends."

"Well, I hope that's true. And don't get me wrong. I'll get by. But I'm trying to tell you what happened to me yesterday—why I messed up. All of a sudden, it seemed as though I had nothing to live for. You know—nothing to hope for. I tried to look ahead, and there was just nothing there to see."

"That's how I felt right after the wreck."

"Yeah. I'll bet you did. But you're young, and everything is ahead of you. You can do things right."

"So can you. You're not old."

"I feel old right now, David." He leaned forward, with his elbows on his knees. "I've been kidding myself. Melissa is just a kid, really, and to her I'm a broken-down old man. I've made a fool out of myself, thinking she might be interested in me."

"I can't have her either, Paul."

Paul looked at David, studied his eyes, and then he nodded. "Yeah. That's another thing we've got in common."

David was relieved to know that Paul was not surprised, that he knew and understood.

"Well, listen, David, what's important now is that we make sure your life goes better than mine has. I want you to tell me what's bothering you—other than worrying about me."

"Mostly, I worry about Arnie taking me away, and sticking me with people who don't even like me." David thought for a time, and then he took a chance. "I think a lot about the future—when I'm grown-up."

"How do you picture it?"

"I imagine myself pitching in the majors. And having my own family. Stuff like that."

"And you'll strike everybody out. Right?"

"Yeah. I mean, maybe I won't. But that's what I like to think about and to hope for."

"Look, David, you really might be better off with someone else. You probably ought to have a mom, and a dad who knows what he's doing."

"That's not how it is, Paul. In all those places I lived, there was never anyone like that."

"So you want to stick it out with me?"

"Yeah."

"All right. I'll try to do a better job. I know I've got to try to teach you the right things. But you've got to try to listen—even if I'm not as smart as I ought to be."

"Okay."

"And David, we've got to play it straight. No stealing reports. No lying. And you and I—we've got to tell each other the truth."

David nodded.

"My old man was pretty much a mess. And now it sounds like yours wasn't great either. So neither one of us really knows how this father thing is supposed to go. I don't even know what to promise you—except that I'll try to do better. That little girlfriend of yours had me pegged about right, I think."

David smiled. "Yeah, but she's got problems of her own."

"It must be going around," Paul said. But then he added, "Look, I'm feeling kind of sick. I need to sleep a little more." And he went to his bedroom.

Later that day, Melissa showed up. She was relieved to find out that Paul was back. David gave her a quick account of what had happened. Everything he said was true, but he left out all mention of her.

"But what brought it all on?" Melissa asked. She walked to the couch and sat down next to David. She was wearing jeans and a navy blue sweatshirt—and no makeup. She was so pretty she took David's breath away.

David hesitated. He wasn't sure what Paul would want him to say.

"Come on. Tell me."

"He's been feeling bad about a lot of things. He thinks he's messed up his life. And then, that guy—John—bothered him."

"Why?"

"You know why."

Melissa leaned back. She put her hand on David's shoulder. "I've seen this coming, but I didn't know what to do. I like Paul a lot, and I want to be friends with both of you guys. I just don't want to hurt either one of you."

"Are you going to marry John?" David was looking straight ahead, not at Melissa.

"Did you like him?" she asked.

"No."

"I could tell that," she said, and she laughed. "Why not?"

"I don't know."

"Tell me, David. I want to know."

"He's not good enough for you. He thinks he's a hot shot."

She laughed even more. "I think you're right, David. I saw that last night myself." She leaned forward and then slid her arm around David's shoulders. "When I was your age, I fell in love with a student teacher at our school. He was handsome and funny and sophisticated. I had dreams that he would fall in love with me and then wait for me to grow up."

David was looking at the floor by now. He knew

what she was saying, and it was embarrassing. But when she didn't say anything for a long time, he finally looked at her, her face close to his. He wasn't exactly surprised to see that tears were on her cheeks.

"David, you won't always feel this way. You'll find the right person for you someday."

He held stiff, looked back at the floor, but he found the courage to say, "I'll always feel the same as I do now."

David heard a little sigh, soft as a bird chirping, and he wanted to turn toward her, but he didn't dare. "Thank you, David. I want you to know how much your love means to me. But trust me, you will feel different about all this as you get older."

David didn't respond, and he bit down hard, gritting his teeth, trying to show no emotion.

After a couple of minutes Melissa took her hand away and reached for her purse. David looked over to see that she was getting out a little packet of tissues. She wiped her eyes. "David," she said, "don't skip any of the parts of life the way I did. Don't miss any of it. Go to the school dances, and be the high school baseball star. Be a kid, and enjoy it. I would give anything to have all that back."

David didn't tell her what he was thinking: that none of that meant anything to him. "Just don't marry that John guy," he said.

"Don't worry. I won't. And I'm going to be your friend forever—no matter what happens. I want you to know that. Do you believe me?"

David nodded.

"I've got to go now. But I'll keep in touch with you

and Paul. Everything is going to be all right. I won't let you down. And Paul won't either."

She reached over and gave him just a brush of a kiss, on the cheek. And then she got up and left.

David slept deep and long that night. He got up late the next morning, on Sunday. Paul had another day off, and he was sleeping late too. David got himself some breakfast, and then he went outside. He took his glove, and he planned to throw some pitches, but he also knew—actually, hoped—that if Lynn heard the sound, she might come out. And it wasn't long before she did. David stopped throwing and sat down by her on the grass.

"Did you and Paul talk things out?" she asked.

"Yeah."

"Do you think he'll be okay now?"

"I don't know, Lynn. I'll just have to wait and see."

"I guess that's all you can do," Lynn said. She looked down, her eyes seeming serious, but when she looked up, she was smiling.

"What's so funny?" David asked.

"Nothing. I'm sorry."

"Come on. Tell me."

"It's nothing. I didn't mean to smile."

"Tell me."

"You just called me Lynn. You've never called me that before."

David was embarrassed. "Oh, I just . . . I don't know . . . I'll call you that if you want me to."

"Does that mean you love me or something?"

"I think it means 'or something.'"

"You give it your meaning and I'll give it mine." She laughed, and David couldn't help but smile.

On Monday, Paul got up and went to work, as usual. But when he came home that afternoon, his voice sounded better—happier—than it had for a long time. He chatted about the hotel, about the busy day, and then he said, "Do you want a Coke?"

David nodded, and Paul got out a couple of cans of soda. David walked to the kitchen and got his, and then the two sat down at the kitchen table.

"I did something I had to do today," Paul said. "A while back I saw an old friend who told me where Kathy was—my first wife. He knew where she worked. So today, I called information, down in California, and I got the number. And I called her."

"Did you get to talk to her?"

"Yup. I think she about fell off her chair when I told her who it was."

"What did you want to talk to her about?"

"I wanted to know how she was doing. And I wanted to hear about my daughters. They're doing all right, considering the start in life I gave them."

"Are they married?"

"Not yet. But my older daughter, Jenny, is getting pretty serious with some guy. Kathy says he's a good man, too. Maybe Jenny will get married and I'll be a grandpa one of these years."

"You could go down there and visit your grandkids," David said, encouraging Paul. All this sounded hopeful.

"That's what I'm thinking. Kathy said the girls have

been asking about me. So I told her about you, and I told her we might take a trip, maybe later this summer, and visit everybody."

"Isn't your wife kind of mad at you?" It was what Paul had always told him.

"Well, I don't know. She seemed impressed that I was trying to raise you. She could have told me what a louse I was, but she didn't. And I told her I would like to make things right to some degree—help with the girls' schooling and weddings and stuff like that."

"What did she say?"

"I expected her to tell me to stay out of her business. But she didn't. She said she would appreciate the help. She acted like she was glad to hear from me."

David saw more life in Paul's eyes than he had seen in a long time. "Is she married now?" David asked.

"No. She was for a while. But it sounds like she found another bum, no better than I was. So she divorced him, too."

"Maybe you could marry her again."

Paul laughed. "Well, I doubt that."

"Didn't you also have a daughter with your second wife?"

"Yeah. And I want to see what I can do to find her, too. But Joan, my second wife, wasn't like Kathy. Kathy was the best thing that could have happened to me. I should have hung on to her when I had her. I just didn't have any sense back then."

"Did you tell her that?"

"Actually, yes. I did."

"Did you tell her that you don't drink anymore?"

Paul looked at the table. "I told her the truth,

David. I said I'd done really well for a long time but that I had messed up a couple of times lately. And I told her I'm not going to drink today."

David looked up, a little surprised.

"That's what you learn in AA. You don't promise anything about forever. You just take one day at a time."

David thought about that, and he did feel some trust. Paul was making sense.

"So, David, I tried to do something positive today. You need to think about doing the same thing."

David looked away from Paul. It was the subject he didn't know how to talk about.

"David, it's not just with me. You need to *join* your team—be part of it. Talk to the guys. Have fun with them. That's what baseball is all about."

"Paul, the guys on the team aren't even talking to me."

"What do you mean?"

David told him what was going on.

"So what are you going to do?" Paul asked.

"I don't know. I was thinking about telling them I was sorry about the stuff I said to Joey, but they won't give me a chance now."

"Can't you tell them before the game tomorrow night?"

David tried to imagine himself doing that. "I don't know," he said. "I don't think so."

"Do you want to go the rest of the year without them talking to you?"

"No."

"Well, then, do something."

"Maybe I can keep saying hello to them and stuff,

and start cheering for them. Then maybe they'll decide to lay off."

Paul finished his Coke, leaning back to pour down the last drops, and then he set the can down. "David," he said, "I made a step forward today. You need to do the same thing."

David thought about that. But he doubted he could say anything to the guys on the team.

chapter 16

On Tuesday night David was pitching. Melissa
called before the game and wished him good luck. "I
can't make it to this one," she said. "But I'll come
again—maybe next week."

Lynn did come to the game, and this time she sat by
Paul.

David's team was playing the Rangers, the first-place
team. Before the game, the coach got everyone together. He stood before the boys, who were sitting on the
grass. "Look, kids," he said, "this is the big game. If we
beat the Rangers, we still have a shot at the championship." He tugged at his cap, and hesitated for a
moment. "But I'm not sure you guys care that much
about baseball. You seem to be more interested in playing other games. I don't like the way you're treating
each other."

The players got very quiet.

"So what do we do about that?"

Everyone knew what the coach was talking about, but no one wanted to say anything. David thought about speaking up, but his heart began to pound, and he knew he couldn't.

"I asked you, what do we do about it?"

"We'll lay off," Cory finally said, and everyone knew what he meant. But that didn't really solve the problem. David knew he had to say something. He took a deep breath, but still the words wouldn't come.

"This team has to work together. It's not just a matter of 'laying off.' It's a matter of supporting each other."

And that's when Joey said, "Tell *him* that. Not us."

And now the tension was thick. If the guys went out on the field feeling this way, David hated to think what would happen. He realized that his hand was going up—as though on its own.

"David?" Coach McCallister said.

"I . . . uh . . ." But his voice had come out so hushed that he knew no one could hear him. He cleared his throat and tried to speak up. "I'm sorry . . . about everything."

"What are you sorry about, David?"

David tried to project his voice, but it still came out as a forced sort of whisper. "I shouldn't have yelled at Joey. And I don't cheer for the guys very much. I had it coming, what the guys did. I'm sorry."

David stared at the grass in front of him. No one moved.

"So is that the end of it, guys?" the coach asked. "David just apologized. What about you?"

"We do too," someone said. David didn't look up, but he thought it was James.

"All right. I think you all know what you need to do."

The coach talked about the line-up after that, and about some strategies. The Giants could run on the Rangers' pitcher, he was convinced. The guy had a very slow move to first. Everyone needed to think about base hits tonight. No one should swing for the fence. It was all the usual stuff, and David was looking at him, trying to be part of things. But he wasn't sure the guys had really forgiven him.

The meeting broke up with some loud yells of confidence, but no one said anything directly to David. He wasn't sure what to do at that point. But when he warmed up, Cory kept yelling, "Good pitch," to him, and that made David feel better.

The Giants were leading off, so after the warm-up, the players headed for the dugout. David was careful to sit on the bench, not to stand by the fence. And he was glad when Cory sat next to him. "Your fastball is popping," he said. David was not at all sure that was true. He hadn't felt that good. But he knew Cory was trying to ease things.

"We've got to change speeds a lot tonight," David said. "These guys are good hitters. I can't just throw fastballs past them."

"If your curve is working, let's use it a lot," Cory said. "Guys don't expect good curveballs in this league."

David liked that. Cory did seem to believe in him.

David was also glad when the Giants got off to a

good start. Jeff fouled off a couple of pitches and worked the count full. And then he walked on a pitch that was up high.

David yelled, with the others, "Good eye, Jeff. Way to get it started." And then he yelled to James to bring Jeff around.

James got a little lucky. He hit a hard ground ball that the shortstop should have handled. But the kid let it hit the heel of his glove and bounce off his chest. Then he grabbed for the ball with his bare hand and missed. By the time he picked it up, he had no play anywhere.

All the Giants jumped up. Some of them gave the Rangers' shortstop a hard time, but most of them were yelling to Dustin to come through. David was right there with the other guys, trying hard to feel part of what was happening.

The pitcher seemed to settle down, however, and he started throwing strikes. On a one-and-two count, Dustin backed away from a pitch he thought was inside, but the ump waved his arm and called strike three.

Cory followed, and he connected pretty well, but he bounced the ball to the right side. The second baseman threw him out. Still, the runners moved up. Now the Giants needed a clutch hit, with two outs.

When the pitcher got two quick strikes on Chase Wright, David was worried the little rally was going to die. He was in the on-deck circle now, and he yelled to Chase to hang in there.

Coach McCallister was yelling, "Come on—just meet the ball."

Chase took a ball, low, and then he did meet the

next pitch. He stroked a line drive to left center, and the runners scored.

David waved the guys around, and then, when they scored, yelled to Chase, "We've got it going now."

As David walked to the plate, he heard all the guys yelling for him. They wanted runs now, and they had let the other stuff go. David could hear Paul, and especially Lynn. She was shouting, "Base hit, David. Keep it going."

David took a pitch that the ump called a strike, and then a ball outside. But he had a feel for the timing now, and the guy was throwing all fastballs. The next pitch was up a little, and David nailed it. He hit a shot to left field.

But the left fielder only had to take a couple of steps. He caught the ball and the inning was over. David was disappointed, but he was glad to have the two-run lead.

When he walked to the mound, he was focused. He wasn't going to force his speed. He was going to hit his spots, change speeds, and keep the Rangers' hitters off stride. He told himself not to think about strikeouts.

He started off the lead-off batter with a good fastball, close to the inside corner. But he didn't get the call. That was okay. He still had the kid set up. He came back with a fastball on the outside edge of the plate. The guy swung weakly and pushed a little ground ball down the first-base line.

James charged the ball, picked it up, and tagged the runner.

David heard his teammates shouting to him. "One down. Good job, David. Keep it up."

David had broken toward the ball, but now he turned back and walked toward the mound. He was almost there before he thought to turn around and say, "Way to go, James. Nice play."

The next batter took a good cut at a low fastball and missed. David came with his first curveball. The ball hung on him, though—stayed too high. The kid swung hard but got under the ball. He hit it high in the air to center field. Brent ran in a few steps, waited, and then realized that he had come in a little too far. He dropped back a couple of steps, quickly, and stabbed at the ball.

And he made the catch. He looked awkward, but he had gotten the job done.

"Nice catch," David yelled to Brent. But he was thinking how close Brent had come to dropping it. And he was thinking what a bad pitch he had made. It was so hard, no matter how much he practiced, to make the ball do what he wanted it to do.

Still, there were two outs, and all the guys were yelling encouragement. "Throw it by this guy, David," he could hear Joey yelling from right field.

David did come with his hard stuff again. He kept the pitch down, and the batter took a hard cut and missed. But the guy was a good hitter. David knew that. He was a guy named Jepson, and everyone said he was on his way to the big leagues someday.

David got the signal for another fastball. He tried to stay outside with the pitch and make Jepson reach for it. But he refused to chase it, and the ump called ball one.

David accepted the sign for a curve, even though he

had messed up the last one. This time his motion was right, and he snapped his release. Jepson was looking for a fastball again, and he tried to jump on the pitch. He got out in front as the ball broke down and away from him.

Swing and a miss.

David felt good now. He went back to his fastball, down again, but Jepson got a piece of it and fouled it off.

So now what? Maybe the curve. Maybe the change-up. But that's exactly what Jepson would be looking for—something off speed. Cory must have been thinking the same thing. He signaled for another fastball, and David nodded. Then he tried to nick the inside corner.

Cory and David had guessed right. The ball was suddenly by Jepson, and he hadn't triggered. The ump was shouting, "Strike three!"

David was out of the inning. And happy. As he walked back to the bench, a lot of the players ran by him and slapped him on the back. "Great job," they were all saying.

Cory ran over to him. "Hey, we got a 'K' on Jepson. That doesn't happen very often."

"We were thinking the same way, every pitch," David said. "Good job."

Cory looked a little surprised, as though he didn't expect David to say anything like that. And David knew he never had before. He even wondered why.

In the dugout, he sat next to Cory again. "You should have heard Jepson," Cory said. "He was *mad*. He said, 'That kid ain't gonna do that to me again.'"

The score was 3 to 0 in favor of the Giants, in the sixth inning. David had been in command all the way. He had had better strikeout nights, but he had never had better control of his pitches. And his defense had really come through for him a couple of times.

David found himself tempted, especially as the game progressed, to slip back to his spot by the fence, where he could think about nothing but his pitching. But he stayed on the bench, and he kept telling guys what a good job they were doing.

In the top of the sixth the Rangers' shortstop blooped a little hit to right field. It would have been a single if Joey had played it right. But he charged too hard and let it bounce past him. By the time he got back to the ball, the runner had trotted in to second base.

David heard James yell, "That's okay, Joey." And David wanted to think that. But he didn't want to lose the game, not after coming this far.

David tried to put something extra on the next pitch, and it sailed on him. When he got the throw back, Cory yelled, "Settle down, David. Just keep popping them in here."

He heard the coach yelling, "Don't overthrow, David."

David knew all that. He stepped away from the mound and rubbed the ball with both hands. He talked to himself. Then he stepped back up, relaxed, and threw a good fastball. The guy swung late and missed.

Then David changed up, and the poor batter swung way ahead of the pitch. David came back with a nasty fastball, low and on the outside corner. The kid flicked his bat at the ball, late. He hit a roller toward second base.

Jeff charged the ball, and so did James, from first. David was taken by surprise. He ran to cover first, but he was late. Jeff grabbed the ball, but there was no one to throw to.

It was a stupid play—sloppy—and David had messed up. He was suddenly angry, especially with himself. He knew he couldn't panic, but he was fighting himself as he walked back to the mound.

chapter 17

David took a deep breath and tried to settle himself down. He had runners at first and third, with no outs, but he still had the three-run lead. He didn't need to get strikeouts. He just needed to throw good pitches and keep the batters off stride. If the batters put the ball in play, he would have to rely on his defense. If the runner on third scored, that was okay. This was not about getting a shutout but about winning the game.

He concentrated on Cory's mitt, and this time he threw with his good motion. He hit his spot, low in the strike zone and on the outside edge. The batter lunged at the ball and bounced it right back to David.

David fielded the ball on one hop. He looked at the runner back at third, and he thought of spinning and throwing to second. But he threw to first and got the sure out. Now he had runners at second and third with only one out.

A strikeout would help right now, but David told himself to relax and throw good pitches. The batter represented the tying run; he was the one David had to keep off base. But a strikeout wasn't necessary. Cory signaled for the curve, and David bent one over the plate. The batter took an off-balance swing and popped the ball up.

Dustin ran in from third base and made the catch, halfway between third and home.

One more out now, and David would be out of trouble. He made a great pitch, on the inside corner of the plate. But the batter fought it off, and hit the ball off the handle of the bat. It arched toward Chase, at shortstop, but it hit the ground and took a flat bounce. Chase got down for the ball, but it skipped under his glove. He ran to the ball quickly, but he came up throwing too hard. He threw wildly, wide of the bag and out of James's reach.

Both runs scored and the runner ended up on second. David walked back to the mound. And now he was worried. The score was 3 to 2 and the runner was in scoring position. The game was on the line.

David told himself not to blame Chase. But his old feeling came back. He wanted to do it himself, get the strikeout. It was the only way to be sure.

He went back to the mound, and he took a deep breath. He told himself not to overthrow. But then he rocked back and fired the next pitch with everything he had. The pitch floated in over the middle of the plate, big as a watermelon.

The batter pasted the ball. He hit it to left field, and deep.

David spun and watched. And then he knew he'd better back up the plate. He spun and ran toward home. But he heard a gasp from the crowd, and then a cheer. He turned and looked back to left field.

Gabriel, somehow, had run the ball down, and he had made the catch.

David couldn't believe it. He had been sure the ball was over Gabriel's head and maybe up against the fence. He could see, from where Gabriel was, that he had run a long way to get to the ball.

"What a catch!" Cory was shouting. And he ran toward the infield to meet Gabriel, who was trotting toward him, grinning.

David followed Cory, and when he got his chance, he slammed hands with Gabriel. "Great catch!" he shouted. Everyone was pounding on the kid, and Gabriel was loving it.

And that was it. The Giants had the lift they needed. They scored another three runs in the bottom of the inning, and then David went out and got the final three outs—a strikeout and two ground balls. The Rangers had two losses now, and they were tied with the Giants again. The Giants still had a chance to win it all.

After the game, Lynn came out on the field and congratulated David. "Do you want to walk home?" she asked.

"No. I've got to stick around with the guys for a while. I promised Paul I would."

"Yeah, that's right. You should. I could . . . oh, never mind. See you tomorrow . . . or sometime."

David could see her disappointment, and he thought of saying, "I'll come by later." But he didn't have the courage. She walked away, and he let her go.

David stayed and drank a soda with the guys. The truth was, he was still uncomfortable, and he would rather have left, but he had to do this. And the players went out of their way to make him feel good about the win. Cory even said, "That took a lot of guts, what you said before the game."

Later, as Paul and David drove home, Paul said, "You did it right tonight, David. I was proud of you."

"If it hadn't been for that catch Gabriel made, we might have lost."

"Maybe. Who knows? But that's true in every game. It's not very often a pitcher just mows everybody down. No one can be perfect all the time."

"I'm just scared that if I can't blow guys away in Pony League, I won't make it to the majors."

"David, who knows? Maybe you'll keep getting better. Or maybe you don't have the arm for the big time. You won't know for a few years, and you can't put all your hopes on baseball."

David didn't like to think that way.

"You're a good student, David. You might be a scientist or a professor—or something like that."

"I want to pitch."

"I know. But just remember, you've got plenty of options. You can do anything you want."

When they got back to the apartment, David had something he wanted to do. "I'll be back in a few minutes," he told Paul.

"Where are you going?"

"I want to talk to someone."

"Who?"

"Just Lynn."

"Don't give me any of this 'just Lynn' stuff. That is one cute girl."

"If you like bones and freckles."

"David, you better take a closer look. In two or three years you'll have to take a number to get a date with her."

"That's what she tells me."

"I don't doubt it. That kid says what's on her mind, doesn't she?"

"Yeah. Too much, sometimes."

"Don't come in too late, okay?"

"You mean like tomorrow afternoon."

"Yeah," Paul said, and he laughed. "Don't ever do that."

But it was strange how sure David felt that he wouldn't have to worry about Paul doing that again.

"I'll see you in a few minutes then," Paul said.

"I might—you know—be half an hour or so. But I won't be too long."

Paul laughed, and that only embarrassed David. So he handed his baseball glove and his duffel bag to Paul, and he took off. When he rang Lynn's doorbell, he was still breathing hard, but he didn't know whether it was from the stairs or from his nervousness. He had never done anything like this.

When the door came open, David was relieved it was Lynn standing there, and not her mother. But now he had to think what to say. "Hi, Pickle," he said, sort of under his breath.

She was stunned. "Hi," she said, and for once, she seemed speechless.

"Do you want to go for a walk or something?"

"Are you kidding?"

"No."

"Check my eyes. Are they open, or am I dreaming this?"

"You look wide awake."

"Oh, wow. This is better than a movie. My fantasies are coming true. Are you madly in love with me yet?"

"Not yet."

"Yeah, well, let's forget I asked that. You're here. That's good enough."

"I just wanted to . . . hang out . . . or something."

"Let's do go for a walk. Like you said. I love walks. If we go for walks together, that's sort of like a date. And if we have some sort-of dates, we're sort of boyfriend and girlfriend, aren't we?"

"Come on, Lynn. I just—"

"Oh, my gosh. You called me Lynn. That's twice. This could be serious. This is like that one movie where—"

"Do you want to go for the walk or not?"

"Oh, yeah. Hey, I'll tell my mom." And she disappeared. But he could hear her, squealing as she talked, and then he could hear her mom and sister laughing. David almost wished he had never started this thing.

But when she came out, she said, "Sorry. You probably heard all that. I'm not too good at hiding my feelings. Maybe you noticed."

"No. It never occurred to me."

They walked on down the stairs and across the parking lot. David thought about telling her what he and Paul had said on the way home, but he was a little embarrassed to bring it up. And so, as usual, he couldn't think of anything to say.

"Okay, here's something I want to know," Lynn said. "You like old movies. So what's your favorite one? I can always tell a lot about people from the movies they like."

"I like that one where a kid hits a ball through a professor's window, and the ball gets some stuff on it so that no one can—"

"Oh, yeah. I like that one, too. The professor becomes a baseball pitcher because no one can hit the ball when it's got that stuff on it."

"Right. Except at the end, he runs out of the chemical because some guy uses it to comb his hair. And he finally has to pitch on his own."

"Yeah. But he wins anyway. Those kinds of movies always have to end that way. And then, at the very end, he gets the girl he wants. Right?"

"Yeah. I think so."

"You remember, all right. That's one of the reasons you like that movie."

David didn't deny it.

"So what's happened to Melissa?" Lynn asked. "Did you decide she's too old for you?"

"No. I always knew that."

"So what are you looking for now? A girl who looks like her?"

"I don't know. Paul—I mean, my dad—said that in a couple of years I'd have to wait in line to get a date with you."

"Really? He said that?"

"Yeah."

"Oh, my gosh. Then maybe it's true. Are you *sure* I'm awake?"

David laughed again, but he didn't answer. The truth was, he still wished that his own dream could come true. "I'll tell you what I wish," he said. "I'd like to be like that professor in the movie. I wish, in one game—in the major leagues—I could strike out every single batter. I call it the *perfect* perfect game. I think about it all the time."

"Why?"

"I just wish things like that could happen. It would be nice if *nothing* would go wrong—even if it was just for that long. Nine innings. And me making it happen—with no one else messing it up."

"David, if you could strike *everybody* out, baseball wouldn't be that fun. That's the whole point. No one can do that."

David shrugged. "Maybe."

"David, if you could have *exactly* what you wanted, would you really want it?"

"What do you mean?"

"I don't know. Stuff just happens. Parents get killed. Fathers go to prison. All kinds of stuff. But it's all sort of interesting, you know? If you could just order up what you wanted, there would be nothing to wonder about. All this stuff happened to me—with my dad and everything—but I got to meet you. And if I'd been over in Bellevue, I wouldn't have."

"You would have met someone else."

"Well, yeah. Maybe. And next year I probably won't even like you. I'll probably be bonkers about some other guy. But I'm still glad this night happened. And you came to my door. It's on my top-ten list—no, about top-three list—of great thrills of my life. And old Dad, stealing money and getting caught—he made it all possible."

David laughed. He wanted to think of things that way—at least try it out. But he couldn't forget all the hurt he had felt over the last three years. If he could order what he wanted, he'd order a father—the kind in the old movies, who always made things right. And he'd keep his mom and his brother, just the way they had been.

But Paul had come along—when he didn't have to. And that was something to be thankful for. Even Lynn had come along as a sort of gift that he hadn't expected—even if she was rather strange.

"Come on, David. Don't do your silent act. Tell me what you're thinking about."

David hesitated, even felt his old resistance. But he stopped himself, and he decided he would try.

ABORTION

Debating the Issue

Nancy Day

—Issues in Focus—

ENSLOW PUBLISHERS, INC.

44 Fadem Road	P.O. Box 38
Box 699	Aldershot
Springfield, N.J. 07081	Hants GU12 6BP
U.S.A.	U.K.

Library of Congress Cataloging-in-Publication Data

Day, Nancy.
    Abortion: debating the issue / by Nancy Day.
        p. cm. — (Issues in focus)
    Includes bibliographical references and index.
    Summary: Discusses the pros and cons of the abortion issue and gives statistics on
abortion in the United States and other countries.
    ISBN 0-89490-645-3
    1. Abortion—Juvenile literature. [1. Abortion.] I. Title.
    II. Series: Issues in focus
    (Springfield, N.J.)
    HQ767.D38 1995
    363.4'6—dc20
                                                            94-40697
                                                               CIP
                                                                AC

Printed in the United States of America

10 9 8 7 6 5 4 3 2 1

Illustration Credits: The Alan Guttmacher Institute from Rachel Benson Gold,
Abortion and Women's Health: A Turning Point for America? New York, 1990, pp.
8, 46, 53, 67; anonymous photographer, pp. 40, 51, 82, 94; Boston Medical
Library in the Francis A. Countway Library of Medicine, p. 19; Christian Action
Council, p. 106; Nancy Day, pp. 27, 58, 78, 86, 91; Tim Haggerty, Advocates for
Life, p. 61; Scott Newton, Planned Parenthood Federation of America, p. 97;
Planned Parenthood Federation of America, p. 22; Geoff Safron, p. 32; Art Stein,
Planned Parenthood Federation of America, p. 100; Jed White, pp. 12, 30, 73;
The White House, p. 110.

Cover Illustration: AP/Wide World Photos.

Contents

Acknowledgments

I would like to express my appreciation to Advocates for Life, the American Life League, the Christian Action Council, the Alan Guttmacher Institute, Human Life International, Gail Miller, the Planned Parenthood Federation of America, the Pro-Life Action League, Dean Stein, Keith Tucci, Jed White, and Susan Zeigler for providing photographs, information, or other assistance. This acknowledgment does not mean that these organizations or individuals endorse or agree with the content of the book—simply that they assisted me in some way. Special thanks to Betty Day, Robert Day, and Joe Sakaduski for valuable help and support. In addition, I would like to express my deep respect and admiration to "Dr. Ed Jones," "Tanya," and "Debbie," who shared their most intimate thoughts and feelings so that readers could better understand this difficult issue.

I have a hard time understanding an attitude of complete confidence because abortion is just about the most extraordinarily complex medical, legal, philosophical, social, and moral issue I have investigated.

—Roger Paynter, *Life in the Tragic Dimension: A Sermon on Abortion*

1

Abortion: The Facts and the Reality

The home pregnancy test was negative. Tanya (not her real name) breathed a sigh of relief and was surprised to find that she also felt a twinge of disappointment. At nineteen, a full-time student living by herself and working, she certainly had no plans to start a family. Three weeks later, she still felt tired and began to wonder. Could she be pregnant after all?

Debbie (not her real name) already suspected she was pregnant. The constant nausea and vomiting were all too familiar. She looked at her two-year-old son. She was twenty-eight and separated from her husband. She didn't want to marry the man she was dating. Being a single working mom was already a tremendous strain. "I'll throw up every day for nine months and then have another baby to care for—no way!" she thought. Then she looked at the home pregnancy test. Positive.

Tanya remembers waiting at the clinic for the test results. "I was sitting there thinking, 'OK, if it's negative, OK, I'll just go on and this time be more careful with everything I do. And if it's positive . . . I'll have a struggle ahead of me.' I kinda felt that I would be alone in whatever I chose."

The results were positive. Tanya cried.

Tough Situations, Hard Decisions

Tanya thought about having an abortion. The baby's father was not someone that anyone would want to raise kids with, she says. She was alone and would have no help. She feared she would be stuck being the mother of a child for the rest of her life and not be able to do anything else. "I didn't want that," she says. Then Tanya considered having and keeping the baby. She talked with a friend who told her how her life would change and how much she would have to give up. Tanya listened. Then she made her decision. "My mamma had just recently passed away and for me it was like a life was taken from me but a life was given to me at the same time." She would keep the baby.

Debbie thought briefly about her options, but she knew what her choice would be. "I was not about to raise another child on my own," she says. "Being a single parent, I needed to work and there was no way I could have worked. Also, my parents would have just died had they known that I was pregnant. . . . I was in no position to have another child—financially, emotionally." She decided to have an abortion.

Who Has Abortions and Why?

Each year, more than six million American women become pregnant. For more than half of them, it is by accident. These are called "unintended pregnancies." About 13 percent of unintended pregnancies end in miscarriage—a "spontaneous" abortion. An estimated 40 percent result in the birth of a child. The remaining 47 percent end in abortion. Two out of three American women will have at least one unintended pregnancy in their lives.[1] And 47 percent of today's women aged fifteen to forty-four will have had an abortion by age forty-five.[2]

Doctors use the word *abortion* to describe the loss or removal of an embryo or fetus before it can survive outside the mother's body. Abortions are classified as spontaneous (occurring from natural causes) or induced. Induced abortions are those in which a procedure is used to intentionally end the pregnancy by removing the embryo or fetus. Occasionally, a pregnancy occurs outside the uterus, usually in a Fallopian tube. These "ectopic pregnancies" are aborted because the fetus cannot survive and will endanger the life of the woman. In discussions on the abortion issue, the word abortion is generally used to mean induced abortions of nonectopic pregnancies.

There are approximately 1.5 million legal abortions in the United States each year. The number has dropped in recent years, declining from an average of 1.6 million from 1980 through 1990. In 1992, the abortion rate was 26 abortions per 1,000 women aged fifteen to forty-four.[3] The ratio of abortions to live births dropped slightly in 1990, indicating that more pregnancies are ending in live births.[4]

More than half of the women who have abortions in the United States are younger than twenty-five. The ethnic distribution is 64.3 percent white and 35.7 percent other races. Unmarried women make up 79.7 percent of the women getting abortions.[5]

7

Unintended Pregnancies in the United States

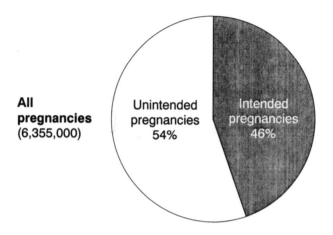

All pregnancies (6,355,000)

Unintended pregnancies 54%

Intended pregnancies 46%

More than half the pregnancies each year in the United States are unintended.

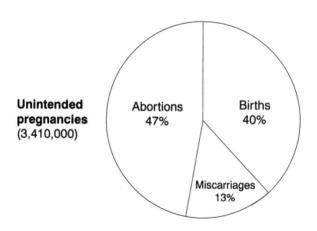

Unintended pregnancies (3,410,000)

Abortions 47%

Births 40%

Miscarriages 13%

Almost half of those unintended pregnancies end in abortion.

About 70 percent of women in the United States who have an abortion want to have children in the future.[6] But, for a variety of reasons, they do not want to continue their current pregnancy. The three most common reasons given are that the woman feels unready for how a baby would change her life (76 percent), that she is not able to afford the costs of a baby now (68 percent), and that she has problems with her relationship with the father or wants to avoid single parenthood (51 percent).[7] About 1 percent of the women having abortions have been advised that their fetus may have a defect and an additional 12 percent fear that the fetus may have been harmed by medications or other conditions. Each year, about sixteen thousand women report that they have abortions because they have become pregnant as a result of rape or incest.[8]

Although 45 percent of hospitals and 24 percent of doctor's offices have abortion facilities, more than 80 percent of abortions are performed in clinics. Fewer and fewer physicians and hospitals are willing to perform abortions. In 1985, 82 percent of all counties in the United States had no abortion provider.[9]

Teenage Pregnancy and Abortion

In 1990, there were about one million pregnancies among American women aged fifteen to nineteen. An estimated 84 percent of teenage pregnancies are unintended. The United States has one of the highest teen pregnancy rates in the Western world. By age eighteen, one in four teenagers will become pregnant at least once. And nearly one in five unmarried teens who experience a pregnancy will become pregnant again within a year.[10]

9

About 21 percent of all abortions are performed on women who are nineteen years old or younger.[11] In 1989, 49 percent of teenage pregnancies resulted in a birth, 14 percent in a miscarriage, and 37 percent in an abortion. About one in four unmarried women under age eighteen who have abortions have never used birth control. For those who have, it is usually one of the less effective methods. Of teenagers who have abortions, three out of four say that they cannot afford to have a baby, and one out of four thinks that she is not mature enough.[12]

Abortion in Other Countries

Worldwide, an estimated 26 to 31 million legal abortions and 10 to 22 million illegal abortions were performed in 1987. Abortion rates vary from 5 per 1,000 women of reproductive age (in the Netherlands) to at least 112 per 1,000 (in the former Soviet Union).

Thirty-nine percent of the world's population lives in countries that allow abortion on request, usually during the first trimester. Most of the rest live in countries that have laws permitting abortion under certain circumstances. Worldwide, about one third of all pregnancies end in abortion.[13]

Different countries and cultures vary in their attitudes and regulations concerning abortion. Abortion only to save the life of the mother is allowed in most Islamic countries, in half of the countries in Africa, in about two thirds of the countries of Latin America, and in three countries in Western Europe.[14] There are varying interpretations of when the woman's life is in danger, and variations, too, in how aggressively the laws are enforced.

In some countries, such as India, abortion for sex selection is common. For cultural and financial reasons, male children are considered more desirable. In Bombay, for instance, less than 1 percent of aborted babies are male.[15]

Access to legal abortion is relatively easy in most Asian countries. Some countries, such as China and Korea, actually encourage abortion (as a way to control their populations) by offering incentives such as paid leave and subsidies. And in some areas, women are forced to have abortions under laws that limit family size.

All over the world, abortion laws and public attitudes continue to change. What remains constant is that, regardless of laws, moral and religious attitudes, and public opinion, abortions continue to be performed. Social worker and author Paul Sachdev comments that "despite fierce controversy, women in all societies continue to practice abortion, legally or illegally, as a solution to their problem pregnancies."[16]

Life Goes On

Debbie told no one of her decision to have an abortion except the man who was the father. "I think it shocked him a bit. But he was supportive. He was the one who took me and helped take care of my little boy and everything." On the day of her appointment, abortion protesters crowded the entrance to the clinic. "It was just god-awful," Debbie remembers. "There were people banging on the car window—that pretty much put me over the edge—people with . . . fetuses . . . dead . . . the whole bit." Debbie is still angry about it. "I mean I was upset enough anyway, but that's just a terrible experience."

11

Abortion has become an increasingly volatile issue.

Tanya, like many people, has mixed feelings about abortion:

> I'm glad I was able to look at it and see that it wasn't for me. . . . It's a choice. It *should* be a choice. . . . For certain situations, it should be there. But just because you happen to make a mistake and you just don't want to live with it, I think that's the easy way out. . . . Now that I'm almost done with my pregnancy, and I feel my baby every day, I don't see how anybody could do it, but I guess people have their own reasons.

Tanya will get support from the baby's father and from her own grandparents. She will continue to work and, at least initially, will also need government aid. "I'm still scared but I have a lot of support," she says, "so I'm glad with my decision. . . . I feel completely comfortable. . . . Life is just too precious. You never really realize it until someone close to you is taken away and then you're given the opportunity to bring life into the world, it's just amazing. And I'm glad I did it."[17] Debbie is comfortable with her choice as well:

> It's a difficult decision. It wasn't an easy decision, especially having a young baby. It's like you look at your young child and realize that, you know, inside you is the potential for that. But—I didn't really feel like I had a choice. I was in no position financially to have another child. And I didn't want to marry this man. . . . To have that child would have taken away from what I could give to the child I already knew and loved.

Debbie is still dealing with the guilt of keeping the abortion a secret from her family and wonders whether she should tell her new boyfriend. But she has no lingering problems or doubts about having had the abortion. "For some people it's a very cut-and-dried decision," she says, "but I'd say that for the majority it's something that people struggle with. . . . I'm sure I made the right decision."[18]

Abortion is a nasty thing, but our society deserves it.

—Margaret Mead [1]

2

Abortion Throughout History

Abortion may seem like a recent issue but abortions have been performed for thousands of years. Throughout history, the discussions people have had about abortion have centered on three main questions: When is a fetus a person? What circumstances, if any, justify an abortion? Who decides?[2]

Ancient Times

References to abortion appear in some of the earliest medical texts. In the fourth century B.C., Aristotle advised "abortion for parents with too many children."[3] Hippocrates (c.460–c.377 B.C.), a Greek physician who is often called the father of medicine, shared his recipes for abortifacients (agents for causing abortion) in his book *Diseases of Women.* Among his recommendations: a head of boiled garlic; a sea scorpion on a wool pad; *elaterium* (squirting cucumber) in double

15

amounts, honey, and wine on a linen pad; butter and alum on coarse flax; and scammony juice, animal fat, barley meal, and wine applied on a linen pad. (The Hippocratic Oath, a modified form of which is still taken by many graduating physicians, was named after Hippocrates, although it is not known who actually wrote the oath. Early forms of it forbade abortion. The oath was not universally accepted by ancient physicians but later became the foundation for medical ethics.)

Egyptians made abortifacients from dung, resin, juniper, leeks, Egyptian salts, and celery seed. Galen (c.130–c.200 A.D.), a physician who wrote many medical texts, described a number of abortifacients, most of them suppositories to be inserted into the vagina.[4]

The first documented opposition to abortion occurred in the early centuries of Christianity. It was a time when Greek and Roman culture routinely allowed abortion and infanticide (killing of infants). The Didache, an early second-century document of Christian belief and practice, declares, "Thou shalt not murder a child by abortion/destruction." Early Christians opposed abortion, based on the fetus's right to life.[5]

The question of whether the fetus is a person was first raised in ancient times. Philosophers Plato and Aristotle both believed that a child had life long before its birth, but that its rights were not as important as the needs of society and family.

The Middle Ages through the Renaissance

Thomas Aquinas (1225–1274), the philosopher and Catholic theologian, wrote that life begins when the soul enters the body, which he said occurred forty days after conception for male fetuses and eighty days after for females. To Aquinas, aborting the fetus before its soul had entered the body was not a mortal sin because life, he felt, did not begin until one had a soul. The standard set forth by Aquinas was adopted by the Catholic Church and remained in effect for centuries.

In later years, quickening—the stage in pregnancy when the mother first feels the baby move—became identified as the time when the soul entered. Abortion after quickening had occurred was considered a sin by the Church and was outlawed in many areas.[6]

Early America

Abortion was legal in the United States until the mid-1800s, but although it was common, it was rarely discussed. Reasons for abortion included health, financial pressures, and covering up the scandal of having had sex outside of marriage. Medical doctors and unlicensed abortionists of varying skill used the same methods: poisons or inserting sharp objects into the uterus. Even with these dangerous techniques, the death rates for abortion were lower than those for childbirth.[7]

Before pregnancy tests became available, it was difficult to determine whether a woman was pregnant or had some kind of menstrual blockage until quickening had occurred. Since doctors treated blockages using the same methods they used for abortions, it is impossible to say when an abortion was intended or how many abortions were performed. This "confusion" was often used as a disguise for abortion. For example, an advertisement from the mid-1800s reads: "Ladies in want of a pleasant and safe remedy for irregularities, obstructions &c., should use Dr. Miller's Female Monthly Powders. It has been said that these powders will produce miscarriage. Without admitting

17

the truth of this assertion, I must confess that it is the inevitable consequence of their use during the early months of pregnancy."[8]

Looking at the birth statistics for the last century, it seems likely that abortions were being performed in large numbers. In 1800, the average American woman had given birth to seven children. By 1900, the number had dropped to three and a half.

Some people have estimated that the abortion rate was between one fifth and one third of all pregnancies. Dr. Edwin M. Hale, a homeopathic leader writing in 1860, said that there is "not one married female in ten who has not had an abortion, or at least attempted one!"[9] Abortion had gone from being the refuge of desperate unmarried women to a form of birth control for married couples.[10]

In 1838, Charles and Anna (Caroline) Lohman, using the impressive names of Dr. Mauriceau and Madame Restell, began to advertise their abortion services in the *New York Herald*. Their venture was a success and they opened branch offices in Boston and Philadelphia. Others imitated them and the performing of abortions became a business.

Then the medical establishment, aided by published investigative reports about Madame Restell, began to express concern over the risks of abortions from unlicensed practitioners. This concern led to the first United States laws regulating abortion. The rising feminist movement also opposed abortion, seeing it as a way for men to conceal the results of their sexual activities.

By the middle of the nineteenth century, the newly formed American Medical Association (AMA) was able to get restrictions placed on abortion. The quickening distinction was dropped and laws were passed to prohibit the advertising

THIRD EDITION—PRICE 6¼ CENTS.

WONDERFUL TRIAL

OF

CAROLINE LOHMAN, ALIAS RESTELL,

WITH SPEECHES OF COUNSEL, CHARGE OF COURT,

AND VERDICT OF JURY.

[REPORTED IN FULL FOR THE NATIONAL POLICE GAZETTE.]

PORTRAIT OF MADAME RESTELL,

Madame Restell was a notorious figure during the mid-1800s. This pamphlet described her trial for a fascinated public.

of abortion services. Individual states began to enact abortion laws.

By the second half of the century, the AMA had joined forces with the Church in an aggressive campaign against abortion, which they called the "evil of the ages."[11] Moral issues were raised and by the end of the century, abortion was illegal everywhere, except to save the life of the mother. Nevertheless, unlicensed abortionists continued to practice and there were few convictions.

During this period, societal fear was growing as women gradually gained rights and independence. The concept of voluntary motherhood—that a woman could choose if and when to have a child—was seen as a danger to family stability. The AMA expressed concern that a woman who sought an abortion was "unmindful of the course marked out for her by Providence. . . . She overlooks the duties imposed on her by the marriage contract. She yields to the pleasures but shrinks from the pains and responsibilities of maternity."[12] The relationship of women's rights to abortion and the issue of a woman's responsibility for the consequences of sex would be discussed for many years to come.

Margaret Sanger

In 1873, the Comstock Law had made it a criminal offense to import, mail, or transport any article or medicine for the prevention of conception or for causing an abortion.

Margaret Sanger, a nurse working in a New York ghetto in the early 1900s, felt that much of the suffering she saw could be avoided if women had access to contraception. She believed that all the other rights that women were fighting for (the right to vote, the right to own property, and so on) would be worthless if they did not have the right to control their own reproduction.

In 1916, Sanger opened a birth control clinic in a poor immigrant neighborhood. She was arrested and imprisoned. The appeal to have her case reviewed led to a ruling that licensed physicians had the right to supply birth control advice to married women for health reasons.

In 1921, Sanger founded the American Birth Control League, which later became the Planned Parenthood Federation of America. Sanger believed that social and economic problems were as valid as medical reasons for birth control.

Eugenics—the desire to improve a race of people—became a movement during this period. Some of its supporters felt that the "wrong" women (white, middle-class, Protestant, married women) were getting abortions and that other, "less desirable" populations were not. Margaret Sanger is quoted as saying, "More children from the fit, less from the unfit—that is the chief aim of birth control."[13]

Pro-choice advocates look back on Sanger as a pioneer in giving women, particularly poor women, access to birth control and abortion. Pro-life advocates feel that her association with the eugenics movement overshadows her other achievements.

The Tide Begins to Turn Again

In the mid-1900s, it was up to doctors and hospital boards to decide when an abortion was required to save the life of the mother. In the 1930s, poverty was a widely accepted reason. In the 1940s and 1950s, some doctors accepted psychiatric reasons.[14] There were few indictments for violations of abortion restrictions and fewer convictions. The safety and availability

In April 1929, after authorities threatened to bar her from speaking, Margaret Sanger appeared in a gag on stage in Boston, while Arthur M. Schlesinger, Sr., read her speech.

of abortion varied widely, with poor and rural women having the least access. In the 1950s, doctors began to complain that hospital review boards were restricting abortions against the doctors' judgments.

In 1959, a society of activist jurists, lawyers, and scholars called the American Law Institute (ALI) suggested that there should be a standard abortion code. The ALI guidelines allowed abortion when pregnancy "would gravely impair the physical or mental health of the mother," when the child was likely to be born with "grave physical or mental defects," and when rape or incest was involved. Each abortion would have to be approved by two doctors.[15]

In the 1960s, the movement to liberalize abortion grew. The National Organization for Women (NOW) included the right of women to control their reproductive lives in the NOW Women's Bill of Rights. Support also came from many Protestant churches.

In 1962, television personality Sherri Finkbine found out that thalidomide, a sleeping pill she had taken during her pregnancy, caused severe birth defects. After talking with her doctor, Finkbine decided to get an abortion in a hospital in her home state of Arizona. Initially, the hospital agreed to the procedure even though in Arizona abortions were officially permitted only to save a woman's life. Then a local newspaper printed the story. In the face of growing publicity, the hospital backed down. Finkbine later went to Sweden to have the abortion. The fetus was severely deformed. Across the country, more than half the people polled supported her decision.[16]

23

A National Ruling

By 1973, thirty-one states permitted abortion to save the woman's life and thirteen states had reform laws modeled on the ALI code. Alaska, Washington, New York, and Hawaii permitted abortion for any reason prior to the point of fetal viability (the time at which the fetus can survive outside the mother). Only Louisiana, New Hampshire, and Pennsylvania prohibited abortion for any reason. But thirty-four states held abortionists criminally liable, and nine also held women who had abortions liable.

Then the Supreme Court ruled in *Roe* v. *Wade* that states could not interfere with the physician-patient decision about abortion during the first trimester (first three months of pregnancy) and could intervene only during the second trimester to ensure safe medical practices that were reasonably related to the mother's health. In the third trimester, states could regulate or even prohibit abortion unless the procedure was necessary to preserve the life or health of the woman.

To people opposing abortion, the Supreme Court decision came like a bolt out of the blue. They were shocked and horrified. Some still call it the darkest day in America's history. Although there were pro-life activists prior to 1973, *Roe* v. *Wade* got the attention of people who had never been active on the abortion issue. Existing pro-life organizations swelled with new members, and new organizations sprang up across the country.

The Organizations

A variety of organizations are actively involved in the abortion issue. Their positions and activities cover a wide spectrum. Planned Parenthood Federation of America, Inc. (PPFA) maintains 900 clinics across the country. According to its annual report, in 1992 PPFA provided contraceptive services to 1.9 million women, cancer screening to 1.7 million women, abortion services to 132,000 women, adoption referrals for 7,600 women, and prenatal care to 7,000 women. It also screens women for sexually transmitted diseases and provides educational services.

The National Abortion Federation was founded in 1977 and works to "preserve and enhance the quality and accessibility of abortion services in the United States." Its membership includes abortion providers, individuals, and organizations active in the reproductive rights movement.

The National Abortion Rights Action League (NARAL) recently changed its name and expanded its mission. Now known as the National Abortion and Reproductive Rights Action League, NARAL is working to achieve, in addition to safe and legal abortion, better sex education, more effective contraceptive methods, wider access to prenatal care, and healthier infants and children.

Other pro-choice organizations (groups that favor allowing women to choose whether or not to have an abortion) include Abortion Rights Mobilization, Catholics for a Free Choice, National Republican Coalition for Choice, Physicians for Choice, Religious Coalition for Abortion Rights, and Voters for Choice.

Another group that supports the availability of abortion is Zero Population Growth (ZPG). ZPG believes that family planning, including abortion, is the only way to slow population growth and to improve the worldwide standard of living.

The largest of the pro-life organizations (groups that oppose abortion based on the unborn child's right to life) is the National Right to Life Committee (NRLC). It is a network of

25

more than three thousand local chapters that work through education, legislation, and political action. According to its literature, the NRLC works to "protect innocent human lives threatened by abortion, infanticide and euthanasia ['mercy killing']."

Human Life International was founded in 1981 by a Catholic priest to "strengthen family life, defend the elderly from euthanasia and protect the preborn." It distributes a wide variety of pro-life materials to more than one hundred countries.

The American Life League, Inc. works to educate the public about pro-life issues, including abortion. It has a strong Christian emphasis and promotes "total protection"—a no-compromise position on the protection of human life from the moment of conception to natural death.

The Pro-Life Action League is headed by Joseph M. Scheidler, who has been called the "Green Beret of the pro-life movement." The organization was a pioneer in the rescue movement—the idea that it is necessary to take direct action to stop abortion.

Operation Rescue (OR) is a coalition of pro-life pastors and laypeople. OR organizes sit-ins at abortion clinics to block patient entry and "save the lives of innocent children." Members also lock themselves in abortion procedure rooms, fill up waiting rooms, or block clinics' outside doors so that no one can get in. Other pro-life organizations include Advocates for Life, Christian Action Council, and Feminists for Life of America.

In addition, alternative or "crisis" pregnancy centers operated by groups such as Birthright and CareNet offer free pregnancy tests, counseling, adoption referral, and other help to women with unplanned pregnancies. These centers support

Crisis pregnancy centers offer support to women who continue their pregnancies to term.

pregnant women during and after their pregnancies and actively encourage them not to get abortions.

In Recent Years

In the last few decades, abortion has become a much-discussed subject. It has been a focal point in selecting justices for the Supreme Court and has become an issue for candidates for state and local offices as well as for the U.S. Presidency.

Some pro-life groups have urged the passage of a Human Life Amendment to the U.S. Constitution, which would grant personhood and constitutional protection to the unborn child. The amendment discussed in Congress in the 1980s stated: "The paramount right to life is vested in each human being from the moment of fertilization without regard to age, health, or condition of dependency."[17] Since 1992, however, with changes in the political climate, most of the effort has shifted toward legislation to restrict abortion and to take action against individual abortion providers.

Many pro-life groups concentrate on church-related activities, support of crisis pregnancy centers, and educational programs designed to convince people to become active in the pro-life movement. They equip others to be "ministers of life," and take the pro-life message into their individual communities.

Other groups choose more confrontational activities such as "sidewalk counseling" (approaching women as they enter abortion facilities and giving them information that may change their minds), blocking clinic entrances, or protesting with picket signs.

In April 1993, the first class of formally trained abortion protesters graduated from a boot camp led by Keith Tucci, a pastor who was then the national director of OR. The students learned how to obtain home addresses and financial information for people who work in abortion clinics. Then they learned how to "lay siege" to these people: praying or picketing in front of their homes, confronting them in the supermarket, and identifying them as "murderers" to their children and neighbors.[18] According to Tucci, the program has been very successful.[19]

Pro-choice activists say that the protesters have gone too far, that they are invading the privacy and threatening the well-being of clinic workers, and that they are interfering with women's access to a legal procedure. Pro-life activists say that these activities are only a small part of the pro-life movement, but that they expect them to continue because they help to reduce the number of abortions that are being performed and thereby save lives.

The escalating violence of the abortion controversy worries many people. Clashes between protesters and clinic workers have become common. Antiabortion protesters say that they have experienced police brutality as well as violent behavior by clinic supporters. Abortion clinic staff members fear the growing numbers of violent acts by abortion protesters. Statistics compiled by the government's Bureau of Alcohol, Tobacco and Firearms show that there have been at least 145 incidents of bombing, arson, or attempts against abortion clinics and other related sites between 1982 and 1993. In 1992 and 1993, a total of thirty-six incidents were reported, with damage estimated at $3.8 million.

Pro-life activists say that the abortion procedure is in itself violent—in fact fatal, to the unborn baby. Some use this feeling to

The abortion issue inflames the tempers of people on both sides of the debate. Here, pro-choice activists make their feelings heard.

counterbalance how far they are willing to go to stop it. While many maintain a commitment to nonviolence, militancy is increasing. Rachelle Shannon, accused of shooting and wounding a physician outside an abortion clinic, wrote in a letter to a pro-life magazine: "Let's pray no one gets hurt, but this is a war and we have to be realistic."[20]

In 1993, Dr. David Gunn, a physician in Pensacola, Florida, was shot and killed by a pro-life advocate because he performed abortions. His death shocked the nation, arousing both cries to keep the pro-life movement nonviolent, and claims that his death had saved many fetuses' lives. A Catholic priest, who was later disciplined by the Church, tried to place an advertisement that advocated the killing of abortion clinic doctors. It was a turning point for people on both sides of the abortion issue. Andrew Burnett, publisher of *The Life Advocate,* wrote in an editorial, "The death of an abortionist [Gunn] has caused me to re-examine my own convictions. Was his life really more valuable than the lives of his thousands of victims?"[21]

Then on July 29, 1994, it happened again. Dr. John Bayard Britton, who had taken over the performing of abortions at the Pensacola Ladies Center after Dr. Gunn was killed, was himself fatally shot on his way to work. He had received threats against his life and had not taken them lightly. He was wearing a bulletproof vest and was accompanied by a security escort, who was also killed. Paul J. Hill, the local leader of a radical antiabortion group called Defensive Action, was arrested, and later convicted of violating federal clinic protection and firearms laws. In his murder trial, Hill provided no legal defense, claiming the shootings were justifiable homicides necessary to save the lives of fetuses. When he was initially arrested, he told the arresting officer, "I know one

31

An arson fire set at the Kalamazoo, Michigan, Planned Parenthood facility on December 1, 1986, resulted in $1.5 million in damage.

thing, no innocent babies are going to be killed in that clinic today."[22]

Britton was not the last. On December 30, 1994, a man went on a rampage, killing a clinic receptionist and wounding three other people. Then he drove to a different clinic, killed another receptionist, and wounded two additional people. While most antiabortion activists condemned the actions of what they called a "deranged individual," others applauded him as a hero.

Abortion rights leaders blame the increase in clinic violence on inflammatory speeches by antiabortion activists, an increasingly war-like atmosphere surrounding the abortion issue, and the willingness of some to do anything to further their cause. They have also asked the Federal Bureau of Investigation to investigate the possibility that a small group of antiabortion militants is involved in a conspiracy to achieve their ends by force. The abortion rights leaders claim that a "campaign of terror" is underway.[23]

Antiabortion forces deny any conspiracy exists and claim pro-choice supporters are exploiting the killings to their own political advantage. They say that every movement has its fringe element, particularly when peaceful means of protest are restricted.

Regardless of what changes, if any, are made in the courts, it appears that the abortion battle has moved to the streets. Both sides acknowledge that the issue is far from settled and that we probably have not seen the end of the bloodshed.

Abortion is a crime that kills not only the child but the consciences of all involved.

—Mother Teresa

3

Ending a Pregnancy

There are a variety of reasons why women have abortions. Whether these reasons are good enough or whether any reason is good enough is one of the many issues that people discuss. Those who feel that abortion is wrong for any reason, at any time, by anyone, do not believe that abortions should be allowed at all. Those who believe that abortion is a woman's right and that abortion should be legal feel that the woman does not need to provide a reason. Between these two positions lies a vast range of opinions. Here is where legislation has often been involved—in permitting exceptions and in specifying conditions under which abortions can be performed.

Mother's Health

One of the exceptions most often discussed is that of the mother's health. Abortions for this reason are sometimes called therapeutic abortions. At one extreme is an abortion that is needed to save the life of the pregnant woman. More common are abortions that are performed to prevent damage to the woman's physical or mental health.

Dr. Frederick J. Taussig, who wrote pioneering books about abortion in the 1930s, divided the medical indications for abortion into three general categories. These were conditions due directly to the pregnancy, diseases aggravated by pregnancy, and anatomical problems that make pregnancy dangerous. These medical situations, he said, compelled the physician to perform an abortion, but only after other kinds of care had proved ineffective.[1] What the role, responsibility, and accountability of the physician should be in such situations is still being debated.

Critics of the mother's health exception say that even if aborting the fetus would save the woman's life, it is immoral to kill one innocent person to save another. They also note that cases in which the woman's life is genuinely at risk are very rare. More common are minor or unproven threats to the woman's physical or mental health.

Fetal Abnormalities

Each year, more than 250,000 babies are born with physical or mental disorders.[2] Prenatal tests can now identify some fetal defects. One of these defects causes Down syndrome. Signs and symptoms of Down syndrome include mental retardation, increased susceptibility to respiratory infections and leukemia (cancer), and heart and other organ abnormalities. Despite these problems, many people with Down syndrome lead happy, productive lives.

35

Another problem that can be detected through prenatal testing is the presence of neural tube defects (problems with the tube that contains the spinal cord). Neural tube defects cause a range of disabilities from little or no handicap, which is rare, to severe paralysis, mental retardation, and early death.

Some women feel unable or unwilling to handle the financial, emotional, and physical burden of raising a severely handicapped child. One study found that more than 97 percent of women who were told of fetal abnormalities detected through an early screening procedure ended their pregnancies.[3]

Abortions for fetal abnormalities are often called "selective abortions." Unlike elective abortion, in which the pregnancy itself is unwanted, in selective abortion a particular fetus is unwanted. This raises the issue of whether it is right to abort a fetus simply because it is defective.

Some say that the ability to control reproduction brings with it a responsibility on the part of parents to be accountable for the life they create. People of this opinion feel that to give birth intentionally to a child with a serious defect inflicts a severe injury on the child.[4]

In some cases, the children involved have agreed. Some have even gone so far as to sue their parents for "wrongful life." Essentially, they are blaming their parents for giving birth to them rather than having an abortion. They argue that they face a lifetime of suffering because of their parents' negligence.

However, picking and choosing among fetuses raises the possibility of a "custom-made" child. Suppose it became possible to detect a tendency toward cancer, obesity, or even left-handedness. The idea of "designer abortions" that would allow parents to search for the perfect baby concerns many people.

Most people would rather live with a defect than not live at all. Many disabled people lead long, satisfying, and productive lives. On the other hand, some conditions are hopeless. Should a woman who knows she is carrying a child that has almost no brain (anencephaly) be forced to remain pregnant and then give birth only to have the baby die? What about babies with AIDS or other diseases that invariably cause suffering and then death?

The principle of nondiscrimination is based on the fact that humans cannot be denied benefits and equal treatment for morally irrelevant reasons. What is a relevant reason for an abortion? Should the penalty for having a disability be death? If all fetuses with defects were aborted, eventually there would be no people with Down syndrome left in the world. Is that necessarily good? One mother of a child with Down syndrome likened it to wiping out a whole race.

Rape or Incest

Another exception that is frequently discussed is abortion for women who are pregnant as a result of rape or incest. Women in such situations may want to abort the fetus because the baby would be a constant reminder of their pain and humiliation. Experiencing the pregnancy would just prolong the victimization, they say. Some women also resist the idea of giving the child up for adoption because they feel under no obligation to the product of a forced union and fear that the child might carry genetic material from a criminally abusive person. And some pro-choice advocates say that if we allow women who have been raped to get an abortion but deny

37

abortions to women who have not, we are punishing women for choosing to have sex.

Those opposed to abortion in cases of rape or incest point out that the fetus is innocent. It cannot help that it was produced by an illegal act and should not have to pay the ultimate price of death for the manner in which it was conceived. Abortion is not a cure for rape or incest and may actually increase the woman's feelings of guilt and add to her victimization, they say.

Sex Selection

In the United States and in most western countries, society's acceptance of abortion for sex selection has always been low. But as families get smaller, a preference for sons as first-born or only children and a desire for "balanced" families, as well as an increasing tendency toward letting women make their own choices, may eventually change this attitude.

It is hard to know how many babies are aborted because they are the "wrong" sex. In this country, women do not need to provide a reason for an early abortion, so no records are available.

In some cases, a sex-linked inherited disease is carried by one or both parents. In these cases, one sex (usually the male) has a strong chance of getting the disease, but the other sex has little or no chance. Parents who know that they carry such a disease sometimes choose to abort fetuses of the susceptible sex. This kind of abortion is actually for fetal abnormality rather than sex selection, because the parents are aborting the fetus solely because of the *threat* of a serious medical condition. However, since such diseases usually affect only some of the children of that sex, normal fetuses may be aborted as well as afflicted ones.

Increasingly, prenatal testing allows parents to find out whether a particular fetus is afflicted. However, some inherited medical conditions do not show up until later in life.

Fetal Development

Much of the discussion surrounding abortion focuses on whether ending a pregnancy is the same as ending a human person's life. To understand the arguments on both sides, it is important to understand the process of conception and fetal development.

About every four weeks, women of childbearing age ovulate, or release an egg that is capable of becoming a human being. The egg passes down the Fallopian tube toward the uterus. The egg contains half of the genetic material (DNA) found in a normal human body cell. Like the egg, each sperm also carries half of the genetic material necessary to create a human being.

When a single sperm enters the egg, a full set of genetic material is produced that contains complete instructions for turning that single cell into a human being. The single cell produced by the egg and sperm is called a zygote.

The zygote completes its trip through the Fallopian tube and reaches the uterus. Now called a blastocyst, it attaches to the inside wall of the uterus. About one in four zygotes fails to implant, resulting in a spontaneous abortion—usually without the woman realizing she was pregnant. One in three will make it to term.[5]

The trip to the uterus has taken six days. Along the way the cell has divided several times and now contains the cells

Much of the debate surrounding the abortion issue focuses on whether ending a pregnancy is the same as ending a person's life.

that will eventually develop into the embryo as well as the cells that will, together with material from the mother, develop into the placenta.

In the second week, the developing organism, or embryo, looks like a flat disk with a connecting stalk that will become the umbilical cord. At the beginning of the third week, the woman misses her menstrual period and may suspect she is pregnant. If left untouched, the embryo now has a 72 percent chance of being born.[6]

Strangely enough, although it has only been two weeks since the egg and sperm joined, most people consider the woman to be one month pregnant. This is because physicians measure pregnancy from the first day of the last menstrual period (about two weeks *before* conception). The distinction between time since fertilization and length of pregnancy is important because in discussions of fetal development and cut-off points for abortion, a two-week difference is significant.

From the second week to the eighth week after fertilization (the fourth to tenth weeks of pregnancy), organ systems develop. The neural tube begins to form, as do the bones, sensory organs, circulatory system, respiratory system, and digestive system. The heart begins beating at about twenty-two days after fertilization. Short webbed fingers form in the sixth week and heart development is almost complete. In the seventh and eighth weeks after fertilization (the ninth and tenth weeks of pregnancy), the embryo begins to move, although the mother can't yet feel it.[7] In its seventh week, the embryo is less than an inch long and weighs one thirtieth of an ounce. Each of its arms is about as long as this exclamation mark![8] At the end of the eighth week after fertilization, the embryo is called a fetus. By

41

now all major systems and external features are established or have begun to develop.

During the ninth through the twelfth weeks after fertilization (the eleventh through fourteenth weeks of pregnancy), the fetus is two to three inches long, its head making up half of the body length. Bone marrow begins to form blood cells, and by the twelfth week, it is possible to tell a male fetus from a female fetus visually.[9]

From week thirteen to sixteen (weeks fifteen through eighteen of pregnancy), the fetus almost doubles in size. The skeleton begins to harden into bone and can be seen on X-ray film by sixteen weeks.[10]

From seventeen to twenty weeks after fertilization (weeks nineteen through twenty-two of pregnancy), the fetus's growth slows slightly. By now, even first-time mothers usually have felt the fetus move for the first time (quickening). The heartbeat can be heard with a stethoscope.[11]

At twenty-five to twenty-eight weeks after fertilization (weeks twenty-seven through thirty of pregnancy), the lungs mature sufficiently for the fetus to be able to survive outside the mother's body.[12] Although new technology has improved premature infants' chances of survival, an infant born at twenty-three weeks has only a slightly better chance of surviving than it would have had twenty years ago. Some scientists feel that there may be a "wall" at twenty-four weeks. Prior to this point, they feel, a premature infant's chance of surviving is very low. After twenty-five weeks, survivability rises sharply.[13]

Methods for Ending a Pregnancy

The most common method of induced abortion is vacuum aspiration. (If performed within two weeks of a missed period, this method is sometimes called menstrual extraction.) It is used in 98 percent of all abortions and to end almost all pregnancies of up to fourteen weeks from the last menstrual period.

The cervix (the necklike opening to the uterus) is gradually dilated, or enlarged. (If the pregnancy is of less than ten weeks duration, the cervix may not have to be dilated.) A thin plastic tube attached to a vacuum aspirator, or suction machine, is inserted in the vagina and passed through the cervix into the uterus. The suction removes both the fetal and the placental tissue, which pass through the tubing and into a vacuum bottle.

A procedure that has become less common (it is used in less than one percent of cases) is dilation and curettage, often referred to as D&C. After dilating the cervix, the doctor scrapes the lining of the uterus with the spoonlike instrument called a curette to remove the fetal and placental tissue.

Often, vacuum aspiration and D&C are combined in a technique known as vacuum aspiration curettage. After vacuum aspiration, the doctor scrapes the lining of the uterus to make sure that all fetal and placental tissue has been removed.[14]

Between twelve and fifteen weeks, either the suction procedure or one of the procedures used for later abortions may be used, depending upon the facilities available.

After the fifteenth week, an abortion may be performed by causing the uterus to contract so that the fetus is expelled, as in natural labor. Contractions are induced with a saline (salt) solution or, more commonly, prostaglandin, a substance that stimulates the uterus. The time from treatment to induction of labor and finally to expulsion can range from several hours to several days. Because this procedure is appropriate only for later abortions, it is used in less than one percent of cases.[15]

All other techniques for abortion account for less than half of 1 percent of the total. These include a technique known as dilation and evacuation (D&E). The cervix is dilated, the fetus is broken apart inside the uterus, and the fetus is then removed through vacuum aspiration. This is becoming more common for abortions beyond the first trimester.

For late second trimester or third trimester abortions, D&E and induction may be performed. The physician injects digoxin, a powerful drug that affects the heart, into the fetal heart to kill it, and then dilates the cervix and induces labor.

A procedure called dilation and extraction (D&X), or intact D&E, is preferred by a few doctors because it carries a lower risk for the mother. For the D&X procedure, the fetus is pulled from the uterus, until only its head remains inside. The doctor then makes an opening in the skull and suctions out the brain, making the skull small enough to pull through the cervix.[16]

A method for late abortions that is rarely performed is the hysterotomy, sometimes called a mini-Caesarean section. It is the most invasive and carries the highest risks.[17] Hysterectomy (removal of the uterus) is very rarely used and is reserved for women who have had a previous indication for hysterectomy.

A recent development is RU-486 (mifepristone), which has been called the "abortion pill." Although the drug is being studied for applications ranging from cancer to glaucoma (an eye disease), it has become known as a medical alternative to the surgical methods of abortion. It has been used in this way in France and China since 1988.

RU-486 works by blocking the action of progesterone, the hormone necessary for the fertilized egg to implant itself into

because they consider them forms of abortion. Some oppose all contraception for the same reason that they oppose abortion—they feel it interferes with God's will.

Although the word contraception implies the prevention of conception, some forms of contraception act *after* the egg has been fertilized. These drugs and devices produce what is essentially a very early abortion.

Sometimes called postcoital contraception (because it is taken after sexual intercourse), the "morning-after" pill is a high dose of estrogen. If taken up to seventy-two hours after the earliest act of unprotected intercourse, it prevents implantation of the fertilized egg. The insertion of a medicated intrauterine device (IUD) up to five days after the calculated day of ovulation also prevents implantation.[20]

The IUD is a device that is inserted by a physician into the woman's uterus; it can remain there for a number of months or years and prevents a fertilized egg from implanting in the uterus. Some IUDs contain hormones or other materials that seem to increase their effectiveness.[21]

Birth control pills work primarily by preventing ovulation. A woman taking the minipill may still ovulate but does not get pregnant because the pill produces changes in the lining of the uterus, the body fluids, and the action of the Fallopian tubes that create an environment hostile to sperm and to conception. Some pills also prevent the implantation of any fertilized eggs.

The Norplant contraceptive implant is a set of six thin capsules, about the size of matchsticks, that are surgically inserted under the skin of the woman's upper arm. The capsules release a low dose of progestin over a period of five years, unless they are removed. The progestin helps prevent ovulation, thickens body fluids to make fertilization difficult, and may also prevent the implantation of any fertilized eggs.

Depo-Provera injectable contraceptive is a single shot that provides a three months' dose of progestin. It also works by making conception difficult and preventing the implantation of any fertilized eggs. Norplant and injectable Depo-Provera are among the most effective methods of reversible birth control.[22]

Of the thirty-nine million American women at risk of unintended pregnancy, nine out of ten use contraception. The failure rates—the percentage of women who get pregnant in the first year of use—for contraceptives range from 85 percent for no method (chance) to less than 0.5 percent (Norplant). Almost half of all unplanned pregnancies occur in women who were using contraception, mainly because of inconsistent and incorrect use.[23]

Doctors' Attitudes Toward Abortion

While many abortion providers feel that they are supplying an important service that women want and are entitled to, some physicians in private practice are uncomfortable with the subject of abortion. Some oppose it morally; others fear the controversy. In an important study of obstetricians' and gynecologists' rationales for accepting or refusing requests for abortion, researchers concluded:

> A major consequence of obstetrical conservatism in the United States has been that women have had limited access to abortion within the traditional health care system; currently, the large majority of abortions take place outside the system in private, single-purpose abortion clinics.[24]

48

Some physicians have built successful businesses on the demand for abortion. They own and run clinics that do huge numbers of abortions and little or nothing else. For these doctors, abortion is a profitable enterprise.

Other doctors work on fixed salaries and do abortions at clinics such as those run by Planned Parenthood. These doctors also provide contraceptives, the diagnosis and treatment of sexually transmitted diseases, and other medical services. Many of them have their own private practices and see their clinic work as a way to help women who can't afford private-practice physicians.

Dr. Ed Jones (not his real name) has been performing abortions at a Planned Parenthood clinic for four years. He says that it is always in the back of his mind that he is terminating a life. "We don't get any great pleasure out of it, but most of us who continue to do procedures realize that there is a need for abortions to be done in a safe, sterile manner and by someone with some competence."

Physicians and staff members at abortion clinics sometimes feel stress from performing abortions. Dr. Jones says that he could not perform abortions every day.

> This can burn you out very, very quickly . . . not so much by the physical labor, as the emotional part of what's going on. When you do an ultrasound, particularly if you have children, and you see a fetus there, kicking, moving, living, doing things that your own child does, bringing its thumb to its mouth and things like that—it's difficult. Then after the procedure, sometimes we have to actually look at the specimen, and you see arms and legs and things like that torn off. . . . It does take an emotional toll.

49

Nevertheless, Dr. Jones feels that the benefit to the patient in terms of her physical and emotional health outweighs the discomfort he feels. He would hate to see a return to the time when there was no one available to perform legal abortions and women were getting infected and were dying from incompetent illegal abortions.[25]

Some doctors have changed their positions on abortion. Dr. Bernard Nathanson was a pro-choice activist and director of the largest abortion clinic in the world, but later altered his views. In a famous statement in *The New England Journal of Medicine,* he announced that he had come to the realization that he had "in fact presided over 60,000 deaths."[26] Dr. Nathanson now opposes abortion and frequently speaks out against it.

Risks of Abortion

Risks associated with abortion include: blood clots in the uterus, which require performing a repeat procedure; hemorrhage (extremely heavy bleeding); tears in the cervix or perforations (holes) in the uterus, either of which may require stitches; incomplete abortion (fetal tissue left inside); a bad reaction to anesthesia; and infection.

Complications are rare when the procedure is performed by a qualified professional in a licensed medical facility. There the rate of complication ranges from one in one hundred (blood clots) to one in one thousand (hemorrhage requiring a blood transfusion).[27]

The risk of injury or death from abortion has declined significantly in recent years. The decline in deaths from illegally induced abortion from 1940 to 1972 was due primarily to the introduction of antibiotics, which could be used to treat infection.

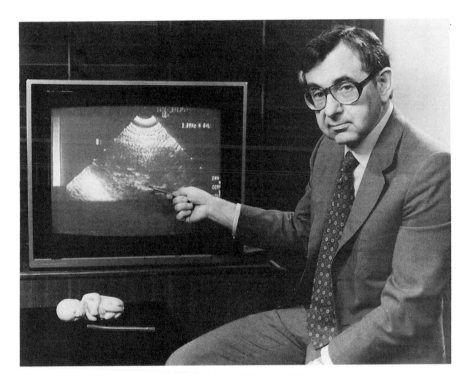

Dr. Bernard Nathanson once performed abortions. Now he campaigns against them.

In addition, the increasing use of contraceptives reduced the need for abortion. Deaths from legal abortion declined five-fold from 1973 to 1985, as a result of increased physician education and skills, improved medical technology, and earlier termination of pregnancies. (The risk of death from abortion increases with the gestational age of the fetus.) The death rate is higher among minority women and women over thirty-five.[28]

It is hard to say whether illegal abortion has become safer or more dangerous since legal abortion has been available. Some people say it is more dangerous because now that physicians can provide abortions in safe settings, illegal abortions are performed only by nonlicensed practitioners or by the women themselves.) Others say that even illegal abortion providers have benefitted from improvements in medical technology and abortion techniques. According to the Council on Scientific Affairs of the AMA, "Regardless of legal status, the critical safety issues are the conditions under which the procedure is done, the safety of the procedure used, the competence of the abortion provider, and gestational age."[29]

Some have suggested that women who have had abortions are at higher risk subsequently for miscarriage, pregnancy complications, and infertility. Researchers from the Centers for Disease Control and The Population Council conducted an extensive review of world literature and concluded that vacuum aspiration (the method used for most abortions) does not pose a measurable risk to future childbearing. Some studies have indicated a higher risk for women who have had more than one abortion or who had complications following their abortion.[30]

Another long-term risk that has been connected with abortion is breast cancer. A seven-year study conducted by Seattle researchers for the National Cancer Institute found that

Abortion-related Deaths

**Number of
abortion-related
deaths in the United States**

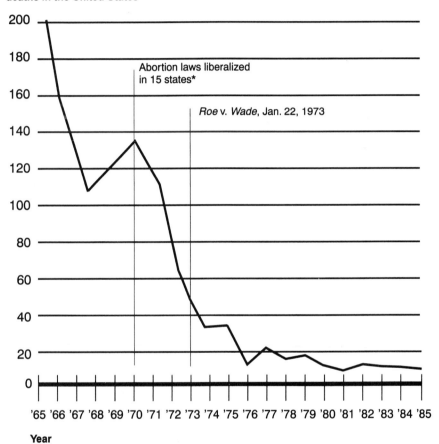

Abortion laws liberalized in 15 states*	
Roe v. *Wade*, Jan. 22, 1973	

Year

*By the end of 1970, four states had repealed their antiabortion laws and eleven states had reformed them.

Abortion-related deaths have declined dramatically since legalization.

an abortion increased a woman's chances of getting breast cancer. The study contradicted earlier research that found no link. The risk was highest for women younger than eighteen and was also higher for later-stage abortions.

The emotional and psychological risks of abortion are hotly debated. Having an abortion, most people acknowledge, can cause feelings of sadness or grief. It can also cause feelings of relief. Women whose religious or moral training forbids abortion or who feel pressure from others not to get the abortion are more likely to suffer mental health problems afterward. So are women who have had previous psychiatric illness.

Women who wanted a child but had an abortion because the fetus was defective have a greater sense of loss than women who did not want to be pregnant. Couples may go through a grieving process similar to mourning the death of a born child and may experience psychiatric and marital problems that require professional help. Siblings, too, may be affected.[31]

According to the American Medical Association, severe emotional reactions to abortion are rare; most women experience relief. Pro-life advocates say that this is untrue. They use the term post-abortion syndrome to describe a cluster of emotional and psychiatric problems that may result from abortion. They liken it to the post-traumatic stress disorder suffered by Vietnam War veterans and say that women may experience flashbacks, nightmares, depression, and other problems for years after the abortion.

Pro-life groups say that post-abortion syndrome is widespread and that their counselors see many women who have long-lasting problems resulting from abortion. The American Psychiatric Association, which compiles information about mental disorders, says that there is no scientific evidence of the condition and that such a syndrome "does not exist."[32]

Not everything that is legal is right, nor should every wrong be legally prohibited; and nothing that is right is right because it is legal.

—P. Ramsey, *The Morality of Abortion*

4

Ethics and Law

There are a number of ethical, religious, and legal issues involved with the subject of abortion. Some of these issues concern the timing or reasons for abortion. Others involve society's views toward sexuality, male and female roles, and concerns about our growing population.

When Does Human Life Begin?

Probably the most frequently debated issue—by people on both sides of the abortion question—is the point at which a human person becomes a human person. It is an important issue because it is often used as an argument against abortion or for setting a cut-off point after which abortion should not be permitted.

When the egg and sperm join, a combination of genetic material is created that has never existed before and will never

55

exist again. That single cell is the start of an individual human life. It carries the blueprint for one, particular, unique human person. But just as a blueprint is not a building, say critics, a single cell (or a zygote) is not a person.

Some argue that human life has intrinsic value; that is, it should be respected just because it is human life. Some people believe that being a member of the human race carries with it special moral significance, and all human beings have the moral right not to be killed. Yet, there is a question as to when that "humanness" begins.

Some people believe that life begins at conception but that humanness or "personhood" occurs later. Until that time, they feel that the woman's right to make decisions about her own body overrides any protection due to the embryo or fetus. In law, a person is recognized as an entity having rights and duties. Under this definition, human beings are not persons until they are born alive. Other cultures have their own definitions. In sixteenth-century rural Japan, for instance, a child was thought of as a human being at conception but only acquired "personhood"—and legal protection—after giving its first cry.

Some people have looked at the issue from the opposite side by examining how we define death. They note that people on life support are clearly human, yet the law in some cases allows support to be cut off to enable them to die a "dignified" death.

The Harvard Criteria, which are used to declare that a person is dead, require that there be no response to external stimuli, no deep reflexes, no spontaneous movements of respitory efforts, and no brain activity. Using the Harvard Criteria, the fetus "surely is not a living human being at the moment of conception and it surely is one by the end of the third month."[1]

During congressional hearings over a proposed human life amendment, scientists argued both for and against the concept of human life beginning at conception. Dr. Hymie Gordon testified that "it is an established fact that all life, including human life, begins at the moment of conception." Other scientists argued that the question is not a scientific one at all. Dr. James Neel stated that "the definition of that moment is a matter of religious conviction, philosophical inclination, or legal necessity."[2]

Religious Issues

Religion has played such a large role in the pro-life movement that freedom of religion has become an argument for keeping abortion legal. (According to the argument, if one group of people hold a particular religious belief, i.e., that abortion is wrong, they cannot force that belief on others by making abortion illegal because that would be violating other individuals' constitutional right to practice their own religion.)

Many pro-life proponents say that it is impossible to separate one's own beliefs from what society should impose. They criticize those politicians who say that they personally are opposed to abortion but feel that the choice should be up to each woman. Bishop James Timlin of Scranton, Pennsylvania, says that this is like saying "I'm personally opposed to slavery, but I don't care if people down the street want to own slaves."[3]

People of some religious faiths look upon the conception of a child as the work of God. A minister active in the right-to-life movement explains that couples may have sex with or without contraception many times without a conception

Religious groups have become increasingly involved in the abortion debate.

occurring. Then, one day, God causes life to be conceived. The couple can no more say that they had the power to begin life than they can say they have the power to end it.[4]

The fundamental religious argument against abortion is that it is up to God to create a human being, to decide whether it should survive, and to determine how long it lives. People who support this argument believe strongly that every abortion destroys one of God's creations.

The Bible contains no mention of abortion. The only passage that comes close is Exodus 21: 22-25, which states:

> When men strive together, and hurt a woman with child, so that there is a miscarriage, and yet no harm follows, the one who hurt her shall be fined, according as the woman's husband shall lay upon him. . . . If any harm follows, then you shall give life for life, eye for eye, tooth for tooth, hand for hand. . .

Other passages from the Bible that have been used to argue against abortion include: "Thy hands fashioned and made me, molded me," (Job 10:8) and "For thou didst form my inward parts, thou didst knit me together in my mother's womb," (Psalms 139:13). These passages indicate that God is the creator and the source of all creative processes. Another example is: "As you do not know how the spirit comes to the bones in the womb of a woman with child, so you do not know the work of God who makes everything," (Ecclesiastes 11:5).

Some people feel that the passage, "Before I formed you in the womb I knew you," (Jeremiah 1:4–5), means that God knows each one of us before fertilization and therefore knows each and every human being who ever was or ever will be (including those lost through abortion).[5]

59

Although the Bible does not specifically prohibit abortion, some Christians believe that it contains messages that should be interpreted as meaning that abortion is wrong. They feel that if an error is to be made, it is better that it be made on the conservative side. In other words, even if we are not absolutely clear about what God wants us to do, we should not do those things we suspect God would not want us to. Others, such as Roger Paynter, pastor of the Lake Shore Baptist Church in Waco, Texas, feel that in cases where the Scripture is not clear, "the final interpretation should be left to each individual person, given guidance within his or her community of faith."[6]

Strong religious feelings fuel many of the people who are working to fight abortion. Judie Brown, president of the American Life League, says, "I would find it impossible to be deeply involved in the pro-life movement if I didn't have religious convictions about when human life begins."[7] Some even see working against abortion as a form of ministry.

The Catholic Church's *Instruction on Respect for Human Life in Its Origin and on the Dignity of Procreation*, published in 1987, declares that "every human being" has a "right to life and physical integrity from the moment of conception until death."[8] The Church's position prohibits not only abortion but any action that is specifically intended to prevent the procreation of children. This includes contraception and sterilization.

The primary Jewish position is that human personhood begins when the baby is born and draws a breath.[9] The taking of the first breath has special significance in Judaism (as it has in some other faiths) because the Bible says that "God breathed into his [Adam's] nostrils the breath of life and man became a living soul." Orthodox Jews generally support a

Bishop Austin Vaughan, from the Archdiocese of New York, addressed pro-life protesters at their first massive sit-in in New York on May 2, 1988.

restrictive position on abortion, while Conservative and Reformed Jews take a more liberal one.[10]

Other religions hold various positions, ranging from opposing abortion under any circumstances to favoring its availability. Some faiths have an official policy and some do not. They also vary in the degree of their involvement in the abortion controversy.

Racial Issues

Operation Rescue distributes a brochure called "Planned Parenthood: Planned Racism." It argues that, since the days of Margaret Sanger, one of the principal aims of Planned Parenthood has been the elimination of the black race. The brochure points out that the abortion rate for black women is much higher than for white women. Some pro-life advocates claim that abortion is a racist tool.

A doctor who works at a Planned Parenthood clinic (and is black) says that most of his patients are white, and he isn't concerned that black women are getting abortions. "It doesn't trouble me," he says, "because I think they do so by choice." He notes that black women also have a higher rate of live births. "Black teenagers are more likely to keep and raise those children than white teenagers are," he says.[11]

Women's Roles, Men's Roles, Society's Role

Imagine that someone holds your child captive and is threatening to kill it. You may not have meant to create the child, but the child (or at least the potential for a child) exists and you are powerless to prevent its destruction. In some people's view, this is the position of the man in the abortion decision. Although pro-choice activists would argue that the fetus has not achieved human personhood, and is therefore not a child, most would agree that the man's role in the abortion decision is a difficult one.

Some people feel that because the fetus is contained within the woman's body and is dependent upon her for survival, and because most of the risks and responsibilities of bearing a child are the woman's, the ultimate decision must be hers. Many men don't stick around when an unwanted pregnancy occurs. Some see making a woman pregnant as a sign of manliness but do not want to accept responsibility for raising or supporting the child that results.

Nevertheless, the man whose sperm created the fetus usually gets no counseling and little support; he may not even be able to discuss his feelings with others because of the woman's desire for confidentiality. In some cases, the man does not even know he has impregnated the woman.

Legal attempts to force male involvement through requirements that the spouse (if there is one) consent to the abortion have failed in the courts. Some people feel that since men are involved in the conception process, they should also be involved in the abortion decision. Others feel that the decision is the woman's and that she may choose—or not choose—to consult the man who impregnated her. While many men are just as happy to be left out of the process, some feel that their feelings *should* count. As one man explained, "Abortion is far too important to be left to a woman and her doctor."[12]

Keith Tucci, who now leads Life Coalition International,

says that when only the woman's concerns count, many people are left out. He says:

> You have a whole group of people, who despise abortion but who are not necessarily pro-life. We have fifteen million women that have lost children. That means you've got fathers, that means you've got brothers, that means you've got boyfriends, that means you've got husbands, and lovers, and all these combinations of people who were not necessarily in agreement with that abortion. . . . You have many women who are post-abortive and are not at all happy about the decision they made. . . . So you've got a whole other element of people who are very unhappy about this whole scenario but more for personal . . . reasons.[13]

Some people feel that the issue of abortion is tied to society's view of women's roles. They see the pressure to regulate or prohibit abortion as another example of our male-dominated culture seeking to control women and to concern itself with women's private lives. They see women caught in a bind between being expected to provide for men's sexual needs and being at risk for pregnancy during a large portion of their lives.

Right-to-life advocates compare our current attitudes toward unborn children to historical attitudes toward women and people of nonwhite races. There was a time when these groups were considered inferior and were treated inhumanely. When we see others as less valuable than ourselves, it makes it easier for us to mistreat or even kill them. Others say that there is no comparison between treating living people cruelly and ending pregnancies that were never meant to begin.

Population Concerns ←

Building the world's population to two billion people took four million years. The next billion took only thirty years. We are adding ninety-five million to our population every year.

Pro-choice proponents warn that criminalizing abortion would increase the world's population by millions every year and that most of the children would be born to women who are not prepared financially, emotionally, or physically to raise them. These proponents note that we are already struggling with pollution, famine, poverty, and the loss of natural resources. Abortion, while not the ideal family planning tool, does help reduce population growth by preventing the births of millions of individuals each year.

Pro-life proponents feel that the issue is the lives of individual children, not the population in general. Some argue that there is no population explosion. Others say that even if there are concerns about overcrowding in third-world countries, letting American women have abortions is not going to help. And, they say, environmental problems are nothing compared with the lives that are being lost *right now.* As activist Judie Brown puts it, "If whales or snail darters were being annihilated at the same rate as human beings are today in our society, there would be massive outrage."[14]

Legal Issues

Legal decisions regarding abortion have focused on two main issues: whether or not the U.S. Constitution grants women the right to abortion if they so choose, and to what extent—if any—the government, in its role as protector of its citizens, should regulate or prohibit abortion.

In recent years, many abortion-related cases have been heard by the courts. Most of these cases concerned individual state restrictions such as requiring minors to get their parents' consent, requiring married women to get their husbands' consent, establishing a waiting period between the decision to have an abortion and the procedure itself, and requiring abortion providers to give women information on fetal development or on alternatives to abortion. Other issues raised by these court cases were individual states setting limitations on where, how, or by whom abortions can be performed, preventing government-funded facilities from discussing abortion as a possible solution to an unwanted pregnancy, and preventing government funds from being used to pay for abortions for poor women.

Reproductive Rights

In *Skinner* v. *Oklahoma* (1942), the Supreme Court invalidated a state statute that provided for the forced sterilization of people who had been convicted two or more times for crimes involving "moral turpitude." The Court characterized the right to reproduce as "one of the basic civil rights of man."

In 1965, *Griswold* v. *Connecticut* challenged a Connecticut law prohibiting the use of contraceptives. The Supreme Court ruled that the Constitution contains a "right to privacy" that protects the decision of married couples to use contraceptives. A 1972 ruling *(Eisenstadt* v. *Baird)* extended the right to use contraceptives to unmarried individuals.

The ruling that first established a national law regarding abortion was *Roe* v. *Wade* in 1973. The case challenged an 1854 Texas statute that made it illegal for a person to perform an abortion or to give a woman something to cause her to

66

Abortions in the United States

**Number of reported abortions in the United States
(in 000's)**

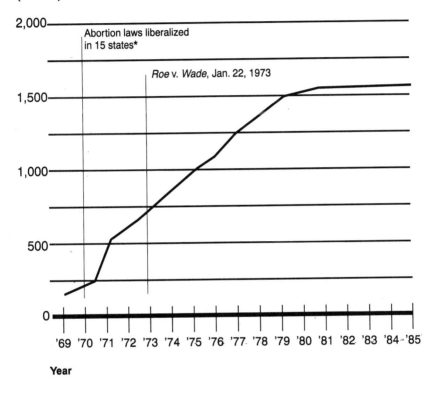

*By the end of 1970, four states had repealed their antiabortion laws and eleven had reformed them.

The annual number of legal abortions in the United States has remained relatively stable in the last several years, after rising rapidly in the first few years following *Roe* v. *Wade*.

abort. Abortion was allowed only to save the life of the woman.

Sarah Weddington, who herself had had an illegal abortion in a "dirty, dusty Mexican border town" after becoming pregnant as a graduate student, was the lawyer who argued the case. It involved a woman whom Weddington referred to as "Jane Roe" to protect her privacy. Jane Roe already had one child, who had been taken away by Roe's mother. She had never finished tenth grade and would lose her waitressing job if the pregnancy continued. Weddington argued that Jane Roe could not afford to travel to obtain a legal abortion and that an illegal abortion would be dangerous and could even result in her death. Weddington and her associate Linda N. Coffee hoped to show that the Texas laws were unconstitutional because they violated Roe's rights to privacy, to safe and adequate medical care, and to choose whether to have a child. They also argued that the laws violated the prohibition of establishment of religion and that they denied Roe equal protection.[15]

The Supreme Court ruled that the Texas statutes were unconstitutional and violated the right of privacy. The Court held that the right to privacy extends to the decision of a woman, in consultation with her physician, to end her pregnancy.

When the Supreme Court agreed to hear *Roe* v. *Wade*, it also agreed to hear *Doe* v. *Bolton*, a challenge to a Georgia law that prohibited abortions except in cases of medical necessity, rape, incest, and fetal abnormality. The Georgia law required that all abortions be performed in accredited hospitals and that two doctors and a committee agree with the woman's abortion decision. The Court ruled that the law was unduly restrictive of the woman's right in the first trimester to decide on abortion in consultation with her physician.[16] It also permitted a broad definition of "health" in deciding when a later-term abortion was necessary for the woman's health. These two rulings established legal abortion in the United States.

Government Funding

In 1977, the Hyde Amendment was passed by Congress. It prohibited government funding of abortions, except when the woman's life was in danger, when the pregnancy would cause severe and long-lasting physical damage, or in cases of rape or incest. In 1981, Congress barred public funding of abortions for victims of rape and incest.

In 1994, government funding of abortion again became an issue. This time, the question was whether abortions should be included as part of a national health care program.

Parental and Spousal Consent

Parental and spousal consent regulations were initially held to be unconstitutional, because the state was giving parents and husbands the right to veto a woman's decision when the state itself did not have that right. Later decisions allowed parental consent (but not spousal consent), if a judicial bypass was allowed. The bypass allowed minors who had strong reasons not to seek their parents' consent to get consent from a judge instead.

Historically, the Supreme Court has allowed different laws and requirements for minors, based on the idea that young people are vulnerable and need protection. Parents are presumed to act in their child's best interests. Some people have pushed for parental notification laws because they feel that the laws will encourage more family communication.

Critics say such laws push young women to get secret and dangerous illegal abortions. Parental notification laws can also delay a young woman's getting an abortion, and later abortions are more hazardous than early ones. Critics also question why the law should specify that parents be informed that a minor is seeking an abortion when it does not require that parents be informed when a doctor determines that a minor is pregnant. Parental notification of a minor's pregnancy would allow parents to participate in the childbirth or abortion decision during the early stages of pregnancy.

People favoring parental notification laws say that parents have a need and a right to know that their child has had an abortion because they are responsible for their child's physical and emotional health. They say that a child is not mature enough to make such a critical decision on her own. Opponents ask how someone who is considered too immature to decide to get an abortion can be mature enough to raise a child.

Regulating Abortion

A key case involving abortion was *Webster* v. *Reproductive Health Services* (1989). It challenged Missouri's 1986 Act that declared that life begins at conception, forbade the use of public funds for the purpose of counseling a woman to have an abortion not necessary to save her life, forbade the use of public facilities for abortions not necessary to save a woman's life, and required physicians to perform tests to determine the viability of fetuses after twenty weeks gestation. The Supreme Court allowed the declaration that life begins at conception to go into effect because five justices agreed that there was insufficient evidence that it would be used to restrict protected activities such as choices of contraception or abortion. The Court upheld the provision that barred the use of public facilities and ruled that the state could implement a policy favoring childbirth over abortion through allocating public resources such as hospital and medical staff. It also upheld the requirement for tests as long as the state did not require tests that would be "imprudent" or "careless" to perform. This decision reopened the door to state regulation of abortion.[17]

Another important Supreme Court case was *Planned Parenthood of Southeastern Pennsylvania* v. *Casey* (1992). It challenged Pennsylvania's 1989 Abortion Control Act which stated that (except in medical emergencies) the woman must wait twenty-four hours between consenting to an abortion and receiving it, that the woman must be given information about abortion and fetal development, that a married woman must inform her husband, and that a minor must obtain the consent—in person at the clinic—of one parent or guardian or obtain a judicial waiver. The Third Circuit Court of Appeals had upheld all the act's provisions except the husband-notification requirement, which was appealed by the state of Pennsylvania to the United States Supreme Court. Although the ruling did reaffirm the validity of a woman's right to abortion under *Roe* v. *Wade*, it revoked the Court's long-standing definition of that right as "fundamental." Instead, it allowed the regulation of abortion so long as the provisions do not constitute an "undue burden" to the woman and said that such provisions are not unduly burdensome merely because they are an attempt to persuade a woman to carry her pregnancy to term.[18]

Laws Governing Protesters

In 1993, abortion providers attempted to prevent OR protesters from disrupting their activities by using an 1871 law, known popularly as the Ku Klux Klan Act, that forbids conspiracies designed to deprive a person or class of persons of their constitutional rights. In *Bray* v. *Alexandria Women's Health Clinic*, the Supreme Court held that the federal statute does not protect women seeking abortions as a class. It ruled that OR was not motivated by class-based discrimination (as the 1871 law requires) but rather by concern for the "innocent victims" of abortion.[19] A later Supreme Court ruling, in 1994, found that the Racketeer Influenced and Corrupt Organizations Act (RICO) may be used to prosecute protesters under certain conditions. Although it is too soon to know what the impact will be, this ruling may severely restrict the actions of abortion protesters.

Antiabortion campaigners say that their activities are covered under freedom of speech provisions. They compare their activities to the civil rights protests of the 1960s and feel that they have a right to make their opposition to abortion heard. In a nationally syndicated column, Joseph Sobran argued that limits on antiabortion protest have closed off the political process. If antiabortion activists are unable to use peaceful means of protest, suggests Sobran, some may resort to violence because they see it as the only option they have left.[20]

Fetal Rights

The legal status of the fetus has a variety of interpretations. In 1946, the District Court for the District of Columbia (*Bonbrest* v. *Kotz*) allowed parents to recover damages on behalf of a child who was injured (by a physician) while still

Legislation has begun to restrict the activities of abortion protesters.

in the uterus. Today, American courts allow claims for prenatal injuries if the child is subsequently born alive. The courts have also allowed fetuses to be considered as persons for the purpose of insurance claims, wrongful-death suits, and vehicular homicide statutes.

The law makes a distinction between a fetus and a not-yet-born child. In most cases, decisions are based on looking back after the child has been born to damage that occurred when the child was a fetus. A child that has suffered a prenatal injury may face a lifetime of suffering and limitation. The law says that such children and their parents should be compensated. Parents who lose a wanted and expected child through an irresponsible action are compensated for their grief and anguish. However, if an abortion is performed before the fetus has the capacity to think and feel, the fetus is killed but not harmed, according to some.[21]

But what about the rights of the fetus? Most of us would choose life over being "killed but not harmed." Is there an acceptable reason for denying rights to a person before he or she is born? A person's *right*, by definition, is something that cannot be denied, conditionally delayed, or taken away by others with more power.[22]

Some people have speculated on the impact of giving fetuses full recognition as persons. They say that it would change how census and population records are kept, and that fetuses' legal rights would change. Four weeks after the *Webster* decision stated that life begins at conception, lawyer Michael Box filed a lawsuit for jailing the fetus of a pregnant inmate without due process of law.[23]

If a fetus has legal rights, should a pregnant woman be allowed to drink, smoke, use drugs, or do other things that affect the fetus? Could a woman be forced to undergo surgery, if it was necessary to save the life or health of the fetus?

In *Grodin* v. *Grodin* (1981), the Court of Appeals of Michigan found that a woman did not have a duty to do whatever was necessary to protect the not-yet-born child but only to behave reasonably during her pregnancy.

Some people worry that the "behave reasonably" guideline is so vague that it could lead to the monitoring of pregnant women's behavior. What is reasonable and who would decide? Virtually every area of a woman's life could come under scrutiny.[24]

Other Ethical Concerns

Medical researchers have determined that certain qualities found in fetal tissue may offer new ways of treating diseases such as Parkinson's and Alzheimer's, which degenerate brain tissue. The idea of using tissue from aborted fetuses raises all kinds of questions. Should a woman be allowed to conceive a child so that she can deliberately abort it and donate its tissue to a relative who has Parkinson's disease? Should women thinking about abortion be told that the fetal tissue could save a life? Should there be a national fetal tissue bank so that fetal tissue doesn't go to waste?

Some people feel that this area of research encourages abortion and that it promotes the idea that the fetus is not a baby but simply excess tissue. They feel strongly that the use of fetal tissue should be banned or at least tightly restricted.

The use of fetal cells might actually *prevent* some abortions. There are well over a hundred genetic disorders that could be corrected before birth by using transplants of healthy fetal tissue. At present, a substantial number of fetuses with these disorders are being aborted. If successful treatments were available, these abortions might be prevented.[25]

The ovaries of a female fetus contain millions of eggs. Fetal ovaries could be transplanted into women born without ovaries, enabling them to have families. Eggs from fetal ovaries could also be used as donor eggs for infertile women. These possibilities raise fresh concerns. The man whose sperm helped create the aborted fetus might have a grandchild and never know it. A child could have a grandmother even though its mother had never been born.

Informed consent (being able to understand and agree to a medical procedure) is a fundamental part of medical ethics, yet the fetus, as donor, can neither give nor deny its consent. On the other hand, organ donations for transplants are frequently authorized by the next of kin on behalf of the person who has died.

Abortion is murder in the moral sense because it is the directly intended taking of human life without justification.

—Charles E. Rice, *No Exception: A Pro-Life Imperative*

Abortion is Murder

People who are fighting to make abortion illegal feel that this issue is a matter of life and death for millions of innocent children. They compare their efforts to those of the anti-slavery activists. They are fighting government bureaucracy, public opinion, and a system that has been in place for many years. And, like the people who fought slavery, they are sometimes willing to break laws to achieve their goals. People who are arrested for their pro-life activities often feel that they are obeying a higher law—the law of God.

Dean's Story

It was a cold, drizzly February day but instead of being at home, spending a lazy Saturday morning with his wife and

Dean Stein and another pro-life supporter try to get the attention of a woman driving into the parking lot of a clinic where abortions are performed.

four children, Dean Stein was out in front of an abortion clinic, carrying a picket sign. He explains his beliefs:

> My father was born and raised in Romania, and when Hitler came in in the Holocaust, there were Christians who risked their lives to smuggle him [my father] and his family out of Romania when it was legal to kill him just because he was a Jew. Today, here we are, across from a Jewish delicatessen that is against us for what we do here. They can't see the correlation. But in the same way the Jews were killed just for being Jews, now babies are killed just for being babies.

As cars drive into the clinic's parking lot, Dean and other picketers shout to the drivers to stop. They hope to get a chance to talk to the pregnant women or to get pro-life literature into their hands. A man who works for the clinic is there as well. His job is to get the women inside the clinic, where the protesters cannot legally go. A car stops. Dean rushes over to lean in the window, ready with his story of heartbeats and hope. The clinic worker rushes over, too, yelling to the driver to get out of the driveway. For a moment, emotion gets the better of them both. A shove here, a threat there. Police are called. Dean goes back to the picket line. He hopes that the information he passed to the woman will work. He hopes she will decide to have her baby.[1]

It's Not a Choice, It's a Child

Human development is a smooth, gradual process. It is hard to identify any point after conception when an immature form of human life is so different from the way it was the day before or the day after that it can be considered a nonperson. Even cutoff points such as sentience (the ability to experience sensations such as pain) don't mean much to pro-life activists.

79

In this country, they note, we do not allow people to kill an innocent person, even if it can be done painlessly and without the victim's awareness.[2]

The issue of the woman's right to control her own body also has limited relevance, say right-to-life proponents. They argue that we only have the right to control our own bodies within certain limits. We can't, for example, protect our bodies by willfully killing other people who happen to get in our way.[3] And even if a woman has the right to control her own body, she does not have the right to control another person's body. As Nancy E. Meyers, media relations director of the National Right to Life Committee, has said, "My freedoms stop where your rights begin. A woman's freedom over her own body stops where another body, another life, begins—the life of her child."[4]

There are many things we can't choose to do in this country. "Ultimately, this is not a debate about whether a woman has a right to choose to get her ears pierced or to have an appendectomy or a hysterectomy," says Meyers. "We are talking about the decision whether to take a human life."[5] By talking about the fetus as a "choice," we are depersonalizing and dehumanizing unborn children. This same technique was used on the Jews in Nazi Germany with tragic results.[6]

Privacy is another issue that troubles pro-life activists. Judie Brown says:

> When people talk about 'keeping legislators out of our bedrooms,' they're trying to imply that abortion is a natural, private part of sex. But killing is not a natural part of sex, and if they were to murder someone in the privacy of their own bedroom, they would be prosecuted under the law. [7]

Does criminalizing abortion—not allowing women to decide for themselves whether it is right or wrong—impose one group's beliefs on another? Pro-life activists argue that right now others are imposing their decision on unborn babies.[8] Who among us would *choose* to be aborted? Most laws enforce someone's morality. Denying abortion does force a woman to carry a pregnancy to term. But the concept of compulsory pregnancy, say critics, is as distorted as labeling life "compulsory aging."[9]

Antiabortion activists have pushed for laws that force abortion providers to show women pictures and descriptions of fetal development. They believe that if women really understood what they were doing, they would not want abortions. Dr. Bernard Nathanson asks, "If the abdominal wall of the pregnant woman were transparent, what kind of abortion laws might we have?"[10]

The issue of abortion is not about choice, say right-to-life advocates. As a pro-life brochure distributed by Hayes Publishing Company explains, the first question to ask is not "Who can choose to do it?" but "Is the action right or wrong in the first place?"

Dependent, Not Disposable

Sidney Callahan, a pro-life feminist, says that "the fetus is an immature, dependent form of human life which only needs time and protection to develop. Surely, immaturity and dependence are not crimes."[11] Handicapped, retarded, and newborn infants are legally protected from harm even though they are dependent and powerless. Why should dependency mean the difference between life and death?

While pro-choice proponents say that we should not bring an unwanted child into the world, pro-life activists argue that

81

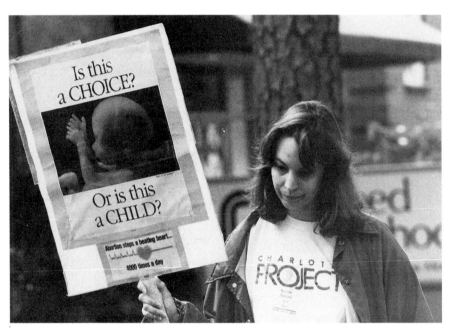

Antiabortion activists often picket clinics where abortions are performed.

the child is already in the world—in its mother's womb. They say that even though the pregnancy is unwanted, the child may be wanted, either because the woman later changes her mind or because an adoptive family wants it. We have no right to impose an irreversible decision on the child that its life is not worth living.[12] And, as John Willke, former president of the National Right to Life Committee, has said, "Since when does anyone's right to live depend upon someone else wanting them?"[13] Antiabortion advocates also reject the claim that unwanted children are frequent victims of child abuse. Abortion, they say, is the ultimate form of child abuse.

Some pro-life activists refer to abortion as the "human holocaust." They point out that while America's wars have caused many deaths, all of the war dead combined do not add up to the number of deaths in the "War on the Unborn," which is estimated to be between twenty-eight and thirty million since 1973 when abortion was legalized.

The Easy "Out"

Some people see the "choice" of abortion as being self-serving. They feel that the woman is so involved (by bearing all the risks and burdens of pregnancy and childbirth) that she is bound to be biased in judging the fetus's right to life. A complex, long-term problem can be solved immediately by a trip to an abortion clinic, but that may not be the best decision. When faced with involuntary pregnancy, say abortion critics, the woman should not be asking "Why continue?" but "Why not?" They believe that human life should not have to be justified, or to prove itself worthy to continue.[14] Abortion never solves the problem, they say, it only complicates it.

The availability of abortion is an easy "out" for the man as well, say pro-life proponents. Men can have sex irresponsibly, knowing that a few hundred dollars can solve any "problem" that results. Abortion exploits women rather than empowers them, they say. As pro-life feminist Juli Loesch has said, "The idea is that a man can use a woman, vacuum her out, and she's ready to be used again. . . . It's like a rent-a-car or something."[15] Women's needs would be better served, say pro-life proponents, by promoting monogamy and commitment than by reducing women to the typically less responsible male style of sexuality.[16]

Many right-to-life activists feel that abortion is a symptom of our lack of morality and responsibility and a sign that we have abandoned traditional values, family orientation, and religious faith. They note that as long as we don't witness the actual dying, the killing of the fetus becomes an option to be weighed only against the relative convenience of other solutions.

Our focus on the prevention of disease at all costs, say abortion critics, steers our conscience, allowing us to abort babies we consider "defective." But what technically can be done is not necessarily what *should* be done.[17]

The Golden Rule says that we should do unto others as we would have them do unto us. Pro-life advocates say that, following this logic, if you agree that abortion is morally permissible, you should ask yourself how you would feel about your mother aborting you.[18]

Saving Babies

Without a law to prohibit abortion, some pro-life activists are working to turn women away from abortion on a one-by-one basis. They stand outside clinic entrances, calling out "Don't kill your baby" and "You don't have to do this." They try to persuade the women that what they are doing is wrong.

Keith Tucci says that turning women away from abortion feels very, very good. "You feel like your efforts are worth it," he says, "no matter what they say about you in the newspaper, or if they sue you, or if they beat you up a little bit, or you spend a couple days in jail, or whatever happens, you feel like 'OK, it was worth it.'" He emphasizes, however, that "the biggest feeling for me is probably humiliation and shame. Humiliation personally and shame kind of corporately for the state of our country, that this even has to happen, that we even have to be here."[19]

According to Joseph M. Scheidler, one of the foremost proponents of pro-life activism, sidewalk counseling is the single most valuable activity that pro-life people can engage in. In his opinion, "counseling goes to the heart of abortion." Scheidler estimates that two or three counselors at each abortion clinic in the United States could save 100,000 lives every year and many clinics would be forced to close.

Critics of pro-life protesters say that they are interfering in women's lives. But Tucci says, "I've never had a woman give birth and say 'I'm really sorry I did this.'" He tells women, "You're not going to be a mother. You *are* a mother right now. You have a baby. . . . Now the decision is, what are you going to do with your baby? . . . Mothers should care for their babies. Or at least, at minimum, give that baby a chance to live."

Pro-choice proponents criticize pro-life advocates for only caring about the fetus until it is born. Protesters work to convince women not to abort their unwanted pregnancies, yet they themselves are unwilling to take on all the babies born as

A young woman prays in front of an abortion clinic.

a result, say these critics. Pro-life proponents argue that many of their members *are* involved with crisis pregnancy centers, adoption organizations, and other groups that provide support to women who carry their babies to term. Keith Tucci believes that:

> We are living under a judicial element that doesn't recognize the unborn person as being a person, so until that can change, we have to save as many children as we can. . . . I can't respect a mother who murders her offspring. It's not a reasonable decision. Murder is not to be respected, especially when it is premeditated murder and you have a hired assassin involved. It's the most brutal and wicked type of murder that exists.[20]

The battle was never "for abortion"—abortion was not what we wanted to encourage. The battle was for the basic right of women to make their own decisions.

> —Sarah Weddington, the lawyer who argued *Roe* v. *Wade* before the U.S. Supreme Court.

6

Abortion is a Woman's Right

Imagine waking up to find that you have been kidnapped by the Society of Music Lovers. They have hooked you up to a famous violinist who needs your kidneys to extract poisons from his blood. To unplug him would kill him. But it's only for nine months. After that, he'll be cured. What is your responsibility? He doesn't mean to cause you any harm. No doubt it would be nice if you continued to help him, but are you obligated to? Judith Jarvis Thomson, professor of philosophy at the Massachusetts Institute of Technology, has used this scenario to illustrate the demands that an unwanted pregnancy places on women.[1]

Gail's Story

Gail Miller was only eleven but she remembers it clearly. The coat hanger. All that blood. She didn't understand it completely at the time; all she knew was that her seventeen-year-old friend was gone forever. Now fifty and the mother of a grown son, Gail looks back on the days when abortion was illegal and some women—like her friend—were desperate enough to try to perform the procedure themselves. Wealthy women could go to other countries or find a discreet private physician, Gail recalls. These options were not available to her friend.

Gail says that, as an African-American woman, she knows what it is like not to have options.

> Growing up in the South, I experienced not being able to have a choice about where I could go to school, where I could eat, where I could put on clothes, where I could go to the bathroom. So the issue is much broader than just reproductive issues for me.

Throughout her adult life, Gail has worked for choice and she became a reproductive health counselor as a result of her strong feelings about people having the power to make their own choices. She emphasizes that choice means that women have the choice *not* to have an abortion as well as to have one. She admits that she doesn't know what she would do if she herself faced an unwanted pregnancy but feels that the choice must be available. "Each person's moral, religious, and ethical values always come into play in that decision," Gail says. "I will continue to fight for choice because I feel strongly about it. The issue of choice has always been utmost in the way I live and in what I hope to accomplish as a human being."[2]

The Right to Privacy

If you discuss something with a lawyer or a doctor, you have the right that that information will be kept confidential. A

Gail Miller addresses the press at a prayer vigil for Dr. John Bayard Britton and his escort, who were shot to death outside an abortion clinic in Pensacola, Florida, in July 1994.

doctor cannot perform surgery on you without your consent, even if the doctor feels it is in your best interests to have the operation. A woman who has a family history of breast cancer and fears that she will get it herself has the right to have a surgeon cut off her breasts, even though they are perfectly healthy and the operation is medically unnecessary. Pro-choice proponents feel that the decision to have an abortion should be just as private and personal.

Supreme Court Justice Louis Brandeis, giving the dissenting opinion in *Olmstead* v. *United States* in 1928, explained the right to privacy as "the right to be let alone—the most comprehensive of rights and the right most valued by civilized men."[3] In *Roe* v. *Wade*, the Court determined that the right of privacy is broad enough to include a woman's right to decide whether to terminate her pregnancy.

Some people worry that if *Roe* v. *Wade* was ever overturned, the right to privacy in other areas would begin to unravel. In particular, they are concerned that contraception could be outlawed, and couples would be unable to plan their families responsibly.

Letting Women Choose

To most pro-choice activists, the fundamental issue is whether anyone—including the government, the Church, and pro-life protesters—can tell women what to do (or not do) with their bodies. Pregnancy carries many obligations, inconveniences, limitations, and even dangers. For women who excitedly await the birth of a wanted child, it is a small price to pay. However, for women who have no dependable partner, or are poor, or too young to responsibly care for a child, or emotionally and physically unprepared to become mothers,

92

the prospect of being forced to continue a pregnancy and then have the responsibility for a child can be devastating. The fact that there have been abortions in virtually every culture throughout history, regardless of the physical risks and societal penalties, shows the strength of women's drive to control their reproduction, say pro-choice proponents. As Charles Hartshorne, emeritus professor of philosophy at the University of Texas, Austin, has said, "There can be little freedom if we lose sight of the vital distinction between moral questions and legal ones. The law compels and coerces, with the implicit threat of violence; morals seek to persuade. It is a poor society that forgets this difference."[4]

Right-to-life activists are attempting to coerce everyone to abide by their view of morality, say pro-choice advocates. In an effort to talk women out of abortion at any cost, they claim, antiabortion activists are deliberately misleading and coercing women. Pro-choice activists cite the "Chicago Method" of sidewalk counseling described in a brochure published by the Pro-Life Action League. The brochure suggests: "When you approach the pregnant woman and her escort, say, 'Did you know about the medical malpractice lawsuits against this place?'" The brochure advises that when the potential abortion client is sufficiently disturbed, "give her literature about an alternative center. . . ." Ideally, it notes, the alternative center should have a neutral-sounding name like "Women's Aid Center" so that women who are undecided about abortion will be attracted to it. The brochure emphasizes:

> It is absolutely vital to the success of the technique that you not disclose that you are an antiabortionist or that the agency you are taking your clients to will not give them an abortion or a referral. . . . If a woman asks you

93

Some pro-life supporters stand at entrances to abortion clinics, trying to persuade women not to have abortions.

whether the alternative center does abortions, say something like 'They'll give you all the help you need. They give abortion information and confidential medical referrals. They'll be glad to talk to you about it, and their services are free.'

This type of deception, say pro-choice advocates, is unfair and unethical. They also criticize the use of photographs that play on the public's squeamishness. In addition, pictures of second- and third-trimester fetuses are misleading, they say, because the overwhelming majority of abortions are performed early, when the fetus is little more than a blot of tissue.

While pro-life proponents accuse abortion clinic workers of talking women *into* abortions, pro-choice advocates say that this is not so. A counselor in a Planned Parenthood clinic says, "I'm very neutral. . . . If I don't feel someone is sure about their decision, I have no qualms about sending them home and saying 'I don't think you're firm enough in your decision. You need more time to think about it.' " The counselor has also escorted women through protesters trying to block the clinic entrance. "It makes me very angry," she says. "I think everybody should have access to medical care without harassment. It's an emotional enough experience and they don't need it to be any worse."[5]

Pro-choice advocates point out that no one is suggesting that anyone should be forced to have an abortion. But when people have such strong and conflicting personal convictions, the only fair solution is to let each person decide for herself. No one should be forced to have, or not have, an abortion.

The Catholic Church has been a particular focus of pro-choice criticism, not just for its opposition to abortion but also for its opposition to contraception. K. B. Welton, author of *Abortion Is Not a Sin*, says:

> Often it appears that in all too many cases the only mission of the Church seems to be to baptize the children and train them to be good Catholics, who will then go on to repeat the same sad experience of not using birth control, getting pregnant at an age when they are unable to properly provide for the child, and thus creating another disadvantaged being on the earth who will most likely require public and private assistance in his or her life.[6]

Fetal Rights vs. Women's Rights

Discussions will continue as to when life begins. What is not disputed, say pro-choice activists, is that the woman is a life, a human being, and a person. Her point of view should start out on at least equal footing with that of the fetus, whose status is arguable, they say. Pro-choice proponents say that pro-life activists are considering the rights of the fetus over those of the woman—forcing her to continue a pregnancy even if it threatens her life or health. This, they say, puts the woman in the position of being a slave to the fetus.[7]

Jane English, who before her death was a member of the Philosophy Department at the University of North Carolina at Chapel Hill, argued that abortion is similar to self-defense from an innocent attacker. Suppose, she suggested, a mad scientist hypnotized innocent people to attack passers-by with knives. You would have the right to kill the attacker in self-defense, even if he or she was innocent. Equally, although the fetus is innocent, it may pose a threat to the pregnant woman's well-being, life prospects, or health.[8]

"How can we justify compulsory pregnancy?" asks human ecologist Garrett Hardin. "Here we are strapping down a living

Pro-choice advocates fight to keep abortion legal, believing the decision should be left for each woman to make for herself.

and breathing creature (the mother) and then forcing her to give birth in the unproven belief that we are saving a 'life.' In many cases we are ruining two lives, the mother's and the baby's."[9] If men were the ones who had to carry the baby for nine months, give birth, and be fully responsible for the child throughout its life, ask pro-choice advocates, what kind of abortion laws would we have?

While pro-life advocates believe that life begins at the moment of conception, pro-choice proponents argue that it is merely the *potential* for life. The potential for life is present in every viable egg in the body of a nun who will never bear a child. Is it wrong that these eggs are not allowed to become human beings?[10] The potential for life is present in almost every sperm a man ejaculates and in the eggs that women of childbearing age shed each month, some of which may have been fertilized yet aborted by nature. None of these forms of potential life are given any special regard, say pro-choice advocates. Even miscarried infants are not given birth certificates, religious rites, funerals, or burials, although infants who die after being born usually receive all of these.

Every Child a Wanted Child

"If we care so little about the birth of a child that we let it happen by accident, and at a time when we are not prepared, or mature enough for the daily and almost lifelong demands of parenthood," said Jane English, "then we need to deeply consider the process of delaying a soul's incarnation into our lives."[11] Some people feel that bringing an unloved and unwanted child into the world is much more barbaric than aborting it. Proponents of this argument say that ending a pregnancy and preventing the birth of a child that cannot be properly cared for shows responsibility, not a lack of responsibility as others have suggested.

What If?

Abortion rights advocates offer a "what if" scenario of what might happen if abortion were once again criminalized. They believe history has shown that women will continue to get abortions, by whatever means they can. Wealthy women may be able to travel to countries that allow abortion. But most women would have three alternatives: bearing the child, having an illegal abortion (most likely from someone other than a physician), or performing the abortion themselves (with or without help). They foresee a return to the IOB (infected obstetrics) hospital wards of the past, where women suffering from the results of botched abortions were treated.

Pro-choice proponents argue that if every woman who faced an unwanted pregnancy continued it to delivery, there would be more than a million additional people in the United States each year. Many of these, born to poor women or extremely young women, would face a lifetime of poverty and disadvantage. Even those born into financially secure situations would face the bitterness of their mother's forced parenthood, growing up in a single-parent home (in many cases), with the lifelong knowledge that they were born only because the law forced their mothers to give birth to them.

Some feminist groups are already preparing for the possibility that abortion could be made illegal by training themselves and others to perform "do-it-yourself" abortions. At a meeting sponsored by a Dallas-area unit of the National Organization for Women (NOW), women saw a thirty-minute videotape that showed how to perform menstrual extraction with a $90

Former Planned Parenthood president and pro-choice spokesperson Faye Wattleton spoke at the April 1989 "Mobilization for Women's Lives" rally in Washington, D.C.

kit containing a glass jar, plastic tubing, and special syringe. "We're being realistic," said Charlotte Taft, an abortion-clinic director who spoke at the meeting. "When abortion becomes illegal, not many physicians will risk losing their licenses. If I have a choice between going to a group of caring women I trust or a stranger, then I'll take the women."[12]

Despite the possible dangers of do-it-yourself abortions, the women say they will do what is necessary. Warns Patricia Ireland of NOW: "The demand for abortion will continue and will be met one way or another."[13] As Cleo Kocol, chairperson of the Feminist Caucus of the American Humanist Association, has said: "Until we have 100-percent safe birth control, until we have men who do not rape, until we have men who never sexually molest their daughters, granddaughters, and nieces, we have need for abortion."[14]

The first right of every child is to be wanted, to be desired, to be planned with an intensity of love that gives it its title to being.

—Margaret Sanger

Alternatives
and Compromises

Although the subject of abortion is complex and generates a wide range of opinions, the nature of abortion tends to make it a black or white issue. Most people have some feelings about it and many people have strong feelings about it. But those feelings tend to fall near the ends of the spectrum. Either people believe that abortion is wrong and there should be laws preventing it, or that abortion is a personal decision with which the government shouldn't interfere. Many people feel that there can be no compromise. Nevertheless, alternatives and compromises have been proposed over the years and people on both sides of the abortion issue continue to debate them.

Limiting Abortion

Some people have attempted to identify critical points in fetal development that could be used to distinguish when abortion is acceptable and when it is not. They feel that such a point should be identified because, although they believe that a woman should have the right to choose abortion, they are uncomfortable with a decision to abort a child shortly before birth. Others feel that there are no critical points. They feel that contraception, abortion, direct killing of an infant, or denying a child food or medical care differ only in the stage of the life process at which parental care is denied.[1]

The problem with setting a cutoff point is an argument known as the logical wedge. The argument goes that a child at birth is not radically different from what it was the day before in the uterus—it simply changed its location. (You don't lose your right to live simply by walking from one room to another.) A fetus the day before birth is not radically different from what it was the day before that. Then the argument can go back, day by day, to conception without finding, on a day-by-day analysis, *any* significant points at which the child changes dramatically.

Critics of this argument note that an independent, air-breathing mammal (the child after birth) *is* greatly different from a dependent, nonbreathing, water-dwelling organism (the child before birth). They also say that the child at birth is radically different from a fertilized egg and that there *are* significant points of development, even if they cannot be pinned down to a particular day. Arbitrary limits exist for voting, drinking, driving, and other rights. A sixteen-year-old is not radically different from a fifteen-and-a-half-year-old, yet a limit must be set somewhere, otherwise we would have to let three-year-olds drive.[2]

Some people suggest that consciousness, the ability to feel pain, brain activity, or some similar criterion be used. One argument places that time at twenty-one weeks gestation, the

103

point when the brain "connects," changing from a collection of nerve cells into a connected machine capable of carrying out human thought.[3]

Better Contraception

Despite remarkable progress in medicine and technology, we do not yet have totally reliable methods to control if and when we have children. Even surgical sterilization, the most effective form of contraception, has a documented failure rate. Failed contraception means unwanted or at least unplanned pregnancies.

The connection between contraception and abortion is a strong one. Margaret Sanger said in 1920:

> The question that society must answer is this: Shall family limitation be achieved through birth control or abortion? Shall normal, safe, effective contraceptives be employed, or shall we continue to force women to the abnormal, often dangerous surgical operation? [4]

Abstinence

Some people feel that many unplanned pregnancies could be avoided if people were urged to abstain from sexual intercourse until they are able to care for the child that might result. By this they usually mean that the couple should be mature and that they should be married. Remaining a virgin until marriage, having sex only with one's own spouse, and abstaining from sex if one is widowed or divorced, are all included within this view. The idea is that because no birth-control method is 100-percent effective, anyone who has sex should be prepared to have a child. People who are married and mature are more likely to be able to handle the responsibility of a child—even an unplanned one.

Genetic Counseling and Gene Therapy

Although prenatal testing has been criticized for increasing the number of abortions by identifying (correctly or incorrectly) infants who will be born with defects, more is being done to correct problems before birth. In the future, it may be possible to identify and treat many fetal abnormalities, thus reducing the number of abortions performed because of fetal defects.

Genetic counseling—evaluating prospective parents' chances of passing on inherited diseases—has become more common. It is possible, in many cases, for couples to know in advance that they carry an inherited disease. These couples can decide whether to have children—before they conceive a child. In the future it may also be possible for parents to conceive only children of the sex that doesn't inherit the disease they carry.

Adoption

In 1986, there were about fifty-one thousand adoptions (by people not related to the child) of American children. About half of these children were older or had special needs such as being part of a sibling group, or having physical, mental, or emotional disabilities. In addition, almost ten thousand foreign children were adopted by Americans that year. (This number dropped to about 6,500 in 1992.) Yet there are still between one and two million infertile and fertile couples and individuals who would like to adopt a child.[5] Some have been waiting to do so for several years.

Although adoption *is* an alternative to abortion, if all the women who have abortions each year decided instead to place their babies for adoption, the number of babies would rapidly

105

Adoption is a frequently mentioned alternative to abortion. This family has four adopted children.

outpace the number of adoptive families. Perhaps if more babies were available, the requirements for adoptive families were loosened, and the process of adoption was less expensive, more families might choose to adopt. It would take a great many adoptive families to absorb over a million adoptees every year.

Many of the people wanting to adopt are waiting for healthy white infants, yet 44 percent of women having abortions are black or Hispanic, and some are carrying fetuses that have defects. Some people are very willing to adopt children of different races or those with special needs. However, it is not known how many of these people still would adopt a special needs child or a child of a different race if a healthy infant of their own race were available.

Not all of the infants who would be born instead of aborted would be made available for adoption, however. It is likely that some children would be adopted by relatives rather than be placed in foster care or institutions. In addition, some women might change their minds and keep their children. And if abortion was unavailable, some people believe that couples might try harder to avoid unplanned pregnancies. No one knows for sure how many infants would become available, how many would be adopted, and what would happen to the remaining children.

Some women feel uncomfortable about giving birth to a child that they will never be able to raise but will continue to think about. Other women who have chosen adoption feel better that they have given a child life, even though they will never be able to parent the child themselves. They feel that they did the right thing, either because they feel that abortion is morally wrong or because they could not bear to abort their own child.

Postnatal Support

Some people feel that if the government and other organizations did a better job of helping women and children, there would be fewer abortions, less child abuse, and a better standard of living for everyone concerned.

Some pro-choice activists have criticized pro-life advocates for fighting abortion but not offering to adopt or otherwise take responsibility for the large numbers of babies that would be born to women who feel unable to care for them. Judie Brown criticizes this attitude by pointing out that no one says to anti-war activists, "You may prevent deaths in a war, but how are you going to feed the people whose lives you save?"[6] However, she agrees that the pro-life movement has a moral obligation, not just to defend "preborn children" but to defend all innocent human beings and see that they are protected.[7]

Christopher Hitchens suggested one possible arrangement in a column in *The Nation.* He says that if we are serious about supporting women and children, we should provide free contraception under a National Health Service which would also guarantee prenatal, nutrition, and health care for any child born to any family. Under his plan, sex education, including contraceptive information, would be part of a national school curriculum. There would be free abortion in cases of rape or incest or if the woman's mental or physical health was threatened; the abortions would be performed by the National Health Service (which would remove any profit motive). Hitchens also proposes a national adoption service supervised by the National Health Service, thereby eliminating adoption rackets and excessive fees. He notes that most of these benefits are already provided by other advanced societies.[8]

The Future

Recent surveys show that the abortion rate is actually dropping. A study by Stanley Henshaw and Jennifer Van Vort of the Alan Guttmacher Institute showed a drop from 1,608,600 abortions in 1990 to 1,529,000 in 1992. Abortions apparently also declined in 1993 and 1994. Reasons for the decline may include less access to abortion (particularly in rural areas), baby boomers aging to beyond child-bearing years, greater use of condoms, more single women keeping their babies, and the influence of antiabortion activists.[9]

The abortion controversy continues. Most people predict additional discussions and legal challenges. A national health plan introduced by President Bill Clinton included abortion services. This angered right-to-life advocates who said they should not be forced to give financial support through tax dollars to something that they are religiously or morally opposed to. Lutherans for Life suggested that pro-life advocates may become conscientious objectors (people who refuse to pay taxes or otherwise rebel because of their religious or moral convictions) if abortion is included in a national health plan. Yet other people note that women's access to abortion is increasingly based on arbitrary factors such as wealth, education, and location, rather than on any moral principle. The people who need it most, they say, have the least access. A national health plan could help to correct that inequity.

People in the pro-life movement continue to work—some quietly through their churches, crisis pregnancy centers, and adoption services; others through protests, active interference, and even illegal acts. Abortion protesters will no doubt continue to do whatever they can to keep the issue of abortion alive.

President Clinton was elected on a pro-choice platform but found that including abortion services under a national health care program created controversy.

Some people think that the solution to the abortion question may lie in some future technological development. For example, an artificial womb which could nurture a fetus until birth would allow women to end their pregnancies without destroying the fetuses. While this would provide an alternative to abortion, it would bring with it the question of what would be done with the resulting babies? Who would "own" them and what would their lives be like? If all abortions became live births, would there be enough adoptive homes for them all? Perhaps the gap could be closed by the invention of a safe, foolproof form of contraception to help reduce the number of unwanted pregnancies.

Deciding for Yourself

There are many strong opinions and deep-rooted beliefs on the issue of abortion. Some people feel that women have an undeniable right to control their own bodies and to make medical decisions that affect their current and future lives. Others feel that abortion is nothing less than the murder of defenseless children. Most people agree that greater individual responsibility would reduce the number of unplanned pregnancies—particularly among teenagers. As a society, we have to decide whether abortion should be available, and if so to whom and under what conditions. By reading materials and talking to people on both sides of the argument, seeking out unbiased information, and searching within yourself for what you feel is right, you will be able to determine your own position. Abortion is certain to be a subject that will be debated for many years to come.

Notes by Chapter

Chapter 1

1. R. B. Gold, *Abortion and Women's Health: A Turning Point for America?* (New York: The Alan Guttmacher Institute, 1990), p.11.

2. The Alan Guttmacher Institute, "Contraceptive Use," The Alan Guttmacher Institute (1993).

3. Stanley K. Henshaw and Jennifer Van Vort, "Abortion Services in the United States, 1991 and 1992," *Family Planning Perspectives*, vol. 26, no. 3 (May/June, 1994), p. 102.

4. Centers for Disease Control, "Abortion Surveillance: Preliminary Data—United States, 1991," *Morbidity and Mortality Weekly Report* (January 28, 1994), pp. 42–44.

5. Ibid.

6. Council on Scientific Affairs, American Medical Association, "Induced Termination of Pregnancy Before and After *Roe* v. *Wade*," *Journal of the American Medical Association*, vol. 268 (December 9, 1992), p. 3237.

7. Gold, p. 20.

8. The Alan Guttmacher Institute, "Abortion in the United States," The Alan Guttmacher Institute (1993).

9. Gold, p. 25.

10. The Alan Guttmacher Institute, "Teenage Sexual and Reproductive Behavior," The Alan Guttmacher Institute (1993).

11. Centers for Disease Control, "Abortion Surveillence," p. 43.

12. The Alan Guttmacher Institute, "Abortion in the United States."

13. P. Sachdev, *International Handbook on Abortion* (Westport, Conn.: Greenwood Press, 1988), p. 12.

14. Ibid.

15. J. P. DeForrest, *No Choice* (Davis, Calif.: Stonegate Publishing, 1991), p. 146.

16. Sachdev, p. 12.

17. Personal interview with "Tanya."

18. Personal interview with "Debbie."

Chapter 2

1. C. Hartshorne, "Concerning Abortion: An Attempt at a Rational View," *The Ethics of Abortion: Pro-Life vs. Pro-Choice!*, eds. R. M. Baird and S. E. Rosenbaum (Buffalo, N.Y.: Prometheus Books, 1989), p. 114.

2. R. Rosenblatt, *Life Itself: Abortion in the American Mind* (New York: Random House, 1992), p. 50.

3. C. Whitney, *Whose Life?: A Balanced, Comprehensive View of Abortion from Its Historical Context to the Current Debate* (New York: William Morrow, 1991), p. 40.

4. J. M. Riddle, *Contraception and Abortion from the Ancient World to the Renaissance* (Cambridge, Mass.: Harvard University Press, 1992), p. 85.

5. T. Stafford, "The Abortion Wars," *Abortion*, ed. J. Podell (New York: H. W. Wilson, 1990), p. 54.

6. Whitney, pp. 43–44.

7. Ibid. p. 44.

8. Advertisement, *Boston Medical and Surgical Journal* LVII (1857), p. 206.

9. R. P. Petchesky, *Abortion and Woman's Choice: The State, Sexuality, and Reproductive Freedom* (Boston: Northeastern University Press, 1984), p. 78.

10. Stafford, p. 56.

11. Whitney, p. 45.

12. Ibid.

13. M. Flaherty, "Norplant and Margaret Sanger's Legacy," *Human Life Review, XIX* (1993), pp. 51–58.

14. Rosenblatt, p. 88.

15. Ibid. p. 89.

16. Ibid. pp. 90–91.

17. M. W. Shaw and A. E. Doudera, *Defining Human Life: Medical, Legal, and Ethical Implications* (Ann Arbor, Mich.: AUPHA Press, 1983), p. 84.

18. Paul Gray, "Camp for Crusaders," *Time* (April 19, 1993), p. 40.

19. Personal interview with Keith Tucci.

20. J. Balzar, "Some fear abortion battle entering more violent phase," *The Charlotte Observer* (October 19, 1993), pp. 1A, 4A.

21. Ibid.

22. William Claiborne, "Abortion foe held in slayings: Doctor, escort killed at Florida clinic," *The Charlotte Observer* (July 30, 1994), pp. 1, 11A.

23. David Johnston, "Is there anti-abortion conspiracy?" *The Charlotte Observer* (August 4, 1994), p. 7A.

Chapter 3

1. J. B. Imber, *Abortion and the Private Practice of Medicine* (New Haven: Yale University Press, 1986), pp. 4, 6.

2. J. A. Boss, *The Birth Lottery: Prenatal Diagnosis and Selective Abortion,* vol. 5 (Chicago: Loyola University Press, 1993), p. 1.

3. Ibid. p. 78.

4. Ibid. p. 3.

5. H. J. Morowitz and J. S. Trefil, *The Facts of Life: Science and the Abortion Controversy* (New York: Oxford University Press, 1992), p. 166.

6. Ibid.

7. S. T. Blackburn and D. L. Loper, *Maternal, Fetal, and Neonatal Physiology* (Philadelphia: W. B. Saunders, 1992), pp. 52–55.

8. G. L. Flanagan, *The First Nine Months of Life*, 2nd ed. (New York: Simon & Schuster, 1982), p. 43.

9. Blackburn and Loper, pp. 52–55.

10. Ibid.

11. Ibid.

12. Ibid.

13. Morowitz and Trefil, p. 166.

14. Imber, p. 58.

15. Ibid. pp. 77–78.

16. D. M. Gianelli, "Shock-tactic ads target late-term abortion procedure," *American Medical News* (1993), pp. 3, 15–16.

17. Imber, p. 78.

18. E. E. Baulieu with M. Rosenblum, *The "Abortion Pill": RU-486—A Woman's Choice* (New York: Simon & Schuster, 1991), p. 17.

19. B. D. Shephard and C. A. Shephard, *The Complete Guide to Women's Health* (New York: Plume/Penguin, 1990), p. 293.

20. J. Guillebaud, *Women's Problems in General Practice*, vol. 24, 3rd ed., ed. A. McPherson (Oxford: Oxford University Press, 1993), pp. 90–91.

21. Shephard and Shephard, p. 42.

22. Planned Parenthood Federation of America, "Norplant Contraceptive Implant," (New York: Planned Parenthood Federation of America, 1993), p. 1.

23. The Alan Guttmacher Institute, "Contraceptive Use," The Alan Guttmacher Institute (1993).

24. Imber, p. 118.

25. Personal interview with "Dr. Ed Jones."

26. B. N. Nathanson with R. N. Ostling, *Aborting America* (Garden City, N.Y.: Doubleday, 1979), p. 164.

27. Planned Parenthood of the Southern Piedmont and Carolina Mountains, "Facts About First Trimester Abortion," Planned Parenthood (1991).

28. Council on Scientific Affairs, American Medical Association, "Induced Termination of Pregnancy Before and After *Roe* v. *Wade*," *Journal of the American Medical Association*, vol. 268 (December 9, 1992), p. 3231.

29. Ibid. p. 3233.

30. R. B. Gold, *Abortion and Women's Health: A Turning Point for America?* (New York: The Alan Guttmacher Institute, 1990), pp. 36–37.

31. Boss, pp. 212–218.

32. Personal interview with American Psychiatric Association.

Chapter 4

1. J. A. Boss, *The Birth Lottery: Prenatal Diagnosis and Selective Abortion*, vol. 5 (Chicago: Loyola University Press, 1993), pp. 123–124.

2. M. W. Shaw and A. E. Doudera, *Defining Human Life: Medical, Legal, and Ethical Implications* (Ann Arbor, Mich.: AUPHA Press, 1983), pp. 317–318.

3. J. C. Callahan, "The Fetus and Fundamental Rights," *The Ethics of Abortion: Pro-Life vs. Pro-Choice!*, eds. R. M. Baird and S. E.

Rosenbaum (Buffalo, N.Y.: Prometheus Books, 1989), pp. 115–129.

4. C. R. Swindoll, *Sanctity of Life: The Inescapable Issue* (Dallas: Word Publishing, 1990), p. 23.

5. J. Brown and P. Brown, *Choices: In Matters of Life and Death* (Avon, N.J.: Magnificat Press, 1987), pp. 5–7.

6. R. A. Paynter, "Life in the Tragic Dimension: A Sermon on Abortion," *The Ethics of Abortion: Pro-Life vs. Pro-Choice!*, eds. R. M. Baird and S. E. Rosenbaum (Buffalo, N.Y.: Prometheus Books, 1989), pp. 143–150.

7. Brown and Brown, pp. 5–7.

8. R. Dworkin, *Life's Dominion: An Argument About Abortion, Euthanasia, and Individual Freedom* (New York: Alfred A. Knopf, 1993), p. 39.

9. Paynter, pp. 143–150.

10. E. Kenyon, *The Dilemma of Abortion* (London: Faber & Faber, 1986), p. 79.

11. Personal interview with a doctor working at a Planned Parenthood Clinic.

12. B. Stout, "Men Should Take Part in the Abortion Decision," *Abortion: Opposing Viewpoints*, eds. C. P. Cozic and S. L. Tipp (San Diego, Calif.: Greenhaven Press, 1991), pp. 79–82.

13. Personal interview with Keith Tucci.

14. Brown and Brown, pp. 5–7.

15. S. Weddington, *A Question of Choice* (New York: G. P. Putnam's Sons, 1992), pp. 50–54.

16. Planned Parenthood Federation of America, "U.S. Supreme Court Rulings On Reproductive Health and Rights," (New York: Planned Parenthood Federation of America, 1993), p. 2.

17. Ibid. pp. 6–7.

18. Ibid. pp. 8–9.

19. Ibid. p. 9.

20. Joseph Sobran, "Paul Hill's dilemma," *The Charlotte Observer* (August 4, 1994), p. 13A.

21. B. Steinbock, *Life Before Birth: The Moral and Legal Status of Embryos and Fetuses* (New York: Oxford University Press, 1992), p. 6.

22. S. Callahan, "Abortion: The Sexual Agenda," *Commonweal* (April 1985), p. 235.

23. Steinbock, p. 103.

24. Ibid. p. 97.

25. S. Begley, M. Hager, D. Glick, and J. Foote, "Cures From the Womb," *Newsweek* (February 22, 1993), pp. 49–51.

Chapter 5

1. Personal interview with Dean Stein.

2. S. Callahan, "Abortion: The Sexual Agenda," *Commonweal* (April 1985), p. 234.

3. J. Brown and P. Brown, *Choices: In Matters of Life and Death* (Avon, N.J.: Magnificat Press, 1987), p. 85–88.

4. N. E. Meyers, "Abortion Should Be Illegal," *Abortion: Opposing Viewpoints*, eds. C. P. Cozic and S. L. Tipp (San Diego, Calif.: Greenhaven Press, 1991), pp. 172–177.

5. Ibid.

6. J. Powell, *Abortion: The Silent Holocaust* (Allen, Tex.: Tabor Publishing, 1981), p. 111.

7. Brown and Brown, p. 85–88.

8. Powell, p. 111.

9. Callahan, p. 235.

10. B. N. Nathanson with R. N. Ostling, *Aborting America* (Garden City, N.Y.: Doubleday, 1979), p. 211.

11. Callahan, p. 234.

12. S. Schwarz, "An Unwanted Child Does Not Justify Abortion," *Abortion: Opposing Viewpoints*, eds. C. P. Cozic and S. L. Tipp (San Diego, Calif.: Greenhaven Press, 1991), pp. 131–136.

13. C. R. Swindoll, *Sanctity of Life: The Inescapable Issue* (Dallas: Word Publishing, 1990), p. 3.

14. Callahan, p. 235.

15. J. DeParle, "Beyond the Legal Right," *The Washington Monthly* (April 1989), pp. 28–29.

16. Callahan, pp. 236–238.

17. P. Ramsey, "The Morality of Abortion," *The Ethics of Abortion: Pro-Life vs. Pro-Choice*, eds. R. M. Baird and S. E. Rosenbaum (Buffalo, N.Y.: Prometheus Books, 1989), pp. 61–74.

18. H. J. Gensler, "An Appeal for Consistency," *The Ethics of Abortion: Pro-Life vs. Pro-Choice!*, eds. R. M. Baird and S. E. Rosenbaum (Buffalo, N.Y.: Prometheus Books, 1989), pp. 93–107.

19. Personal interview with Keith Tucci.

20. Ibid.

Chapter 6

1. J. J. Thomson, "A Defense of Abortion," *The Ethics of Abortion: Pro-Life vs. Pro-Choice!*, eds. R. M. Baird and S. E. Rosenbaum (Buffalo, N.Y.: Prometheus Books, 1989), pp. 29–44.

2. Personal interview with Gail Miller.

3. L. H. Tribe, *Abortion: The Clash of Absolutes* (New York: W. W. Norton, 1992), p. 92.

4. C. Hartshorne, *The Ethics of Abortion: Pro-Life vs. Pro-Choice!*, eds. R. M. Baird and S. E. Rosenbaum (Buffalo, N.Y.: Prometheus Books, 1989), pp. 109–114.

5. Personal interview with a Planned Parenthood counselor.

6. K. B. Welton, "An Unwanted Child Justifies Abortion," *Abortion: Opposing Viewpoints*, eds. C. P. Cozic and S. L. Tipp (San Diego, Calif.: Greenhaven Press, 1991), pp. 124–130.

7. Ibid.

8. J. English, "Abortion and the Concept of a Person," *The Ethics of Abortion: Pro-Life vs. Pro-Choice!*, eds. R. M. Baird and S. E. Rosenbaum (Buffalo, N.Y.: Prometheus Books, 1989), pp. 83–92.

9. Welton, p. 129.

10. Hartshorne, pp. 109–114.

11. Welton, p. 126.

12. A. Toufexis, "Abortions Without Doctors," *Abortion*, vol 62, ed. J. Podell (New York: H. W. Wilson, 1990), p. 129.

13. Ibid.

14. C. Kocol, "Let's Take the Guilt Away," *Abortion*, vol. 62, ed. J. Podell (New York: H. W. Wilson, 1990).

Chapter 7

1. J. P. DeForrest, *No Choice* (Davis, Calif.: Stonegate Publishing, 1991), p. 10.

2. J. C. Callahan, *The Ethics of Abortion: Pro-Life vs. Pro-Choice!*, eds. R. M. Baird and S. E. Rosenbaum (Buffalo, N.Y.: Prometheus Books, 1989), pp. 115–129.

3. H. J. Morowitz and J. S. Trefil, *The Facts of Life: Science and the Abortion Controversy* (New York: Oxford University Press, 1992), p. 117.

4. R. P. Petchesky, *Abortion and Woman's Choice: The State, Sexuality, and Reproductive Freedom* (Boston: Northeastern University Press, 1984), p. 91.

5. National Council For Adoption, "Fact Sheet on Adoption," (1993).

6. J. Brown and P. Brown, *Choices: In Matters of Life and Death* (Avon, N.J.: Magnificat Press, 1987), pp. 9, 125.

7. Ibid.

8. C. Hitchens, "Minority Report," *The Nation*, vol. 248 (April 24, 1989), p. 546.

9. Jean Seligmann, "On Demand = Less Demand," *Newsweek* (June 27, 1994), p. 49.

Glossary

abortifacient—(ah-bort-i-FAY-shent)—An agent that produces an abortion.

abortion—The ending of a pregnancy before the fetus can survive outside the woman's body (usually prior to 22 weeks gestation or when fetal weight is less than 500 grams).

abortionist—Someone who performs abortions.

alternative pregnancy centers—Places that provide prenatal and postnatal support to pregnant women as an alternative to abortion. These centers counsel women against abortion, instead referring them to adoption services if they do not want to keep the baby.

blastocyst—The embryonic stage in which the fertilized egg has become a hollow cluster of cells.

conception—The fertilization of an egg by a sperm.

contraception—The use of drugs, devices, or other methods to prevent pregnancy.

crisis pregnancy centers—See alternative pregnancy centers.

dilation and curettage (D&C)—Enlarging the cervix and scraping the inside of the uterus.

dilation and evacuation (D&E)—Enlarging the cervix and removing the products of conception (fertilized egg, embryo, or fetus, and placental tissue).

ectopic pregnancy—A pregnancy outside the uterus.

elective abortion—An abortion that is not necessary to save the life of the mother.

embryo—The developing organism, in humans, from conception until about the end of the second month.

eugenics—Practices and policies designed to improve the hereditary qualities of a race of people.

fetus—The product of conception from the end of the eighth week to the moment of birth.

gestation—The *term* (period of time) of pregnancy.

illegal abortion—An abortion performed by the woman herself or by someone who is neither a licensed physician nor being immediately supervised by a licensed physician.

induced abortion—A procedure intended to end a suspected or known uterine pregnancy and to produce a nonviable fetus at any gestational age.

induced labor—Bringing about the process of expulsion of the fetus and placenta from the uterus.

legal abortion—An abortion performed by a licensed physician or someone acting under the immediate supervision of a licensed physician within the guidelines established by state or national law.

menstrual extraction—Using vacuum aspiration to produce an abortion in the very early stages of pregnancy.

parental consent—The requirement that one or both parents give (usually written) approval before a minor can obtain an abortion.

pro-choice—The belief that women have the right to have an abortion if they want one.

pro-life—The belief that all human life should be protected by law, including the unborn, the elderly, the terminally ill, and the disabled; and that abortion, assisted suicide, and euthanasia should not be permitted.

quickening—The point in a pregnancy at which the mother feels the baby move for the first time (usually in the fourth month).

right to life—Opposition to abortion based upon the belief that a fetus or embryo is entitled to life, usually from the time of conception.

selective abortion—An abortion performed to end a particular pregnancy, usually because of fetal defects, not because the pregnancy was unwanted.

spousal consent—The requirement that a husband or wife give (usually written) approval before the other spouse can proceed with an action—in this case, the requirement that a husband agree that his wife can have an abortion.

thalidomide—A drug that, when taken during pregnancy, can produce severe birth defects.

trimester—One of the three 3-month periods into which the term of pregnancy is divided.

vacuum aspiration—An abortion procedure using suction to remove the fetal and placental tissue.

viability—The point at which the fetus can survive outside the mother's body—usually from 23 to 25 weeks gestation.

waiting period—The requirement that a woman must wait for a specific period, either between the time she seeks an abortion and has one, or between the time she receives counseling and has the abortion.

women's health centers—Clinics that offer medical services to women, often at reduced or income-based charges. Most offer abortion services in addition to prenatal care, contraceptive services, cancer screening, and other medical services.

Further Reading

Caruana, Claudia. *The Abortion Debate.* Brookfield, Conn.: Millbrook Press, 1992.

Cozic, Charles P., and Stacey L. Tipp. *Abortion: Opposing Viewpoints.* San Diego, Calif.: Greenhaven Press, 1991.

Emmens, Carol A. *The Abortion Controversy.* New York: Julian Messner, 1991.

Wharton, Mandy. *Abortion.* New York: Gloucester Press, 1989.

Winikoff, Beverly, and Suzanne Wymelenberg. *The Contraceptive Handbook: A Guide to Safe and Effective Choices.* Yonkers, N.Y.: Consumer Reports Books, 1992.

Index

126